SCAR COUNTY SHOWDOWN

When town marshal Arthur Curry is gunned down from behind by killers unknown, his brother, Sam, comes to Columbus to pay his last respects and to seek vengeance. The mayor, an old friend of Sam's, believes he knows who is responsible for the murderous crime. But Sam makes his own investigations, which lead him headfirst into a nightmare to which there is no easy solution. Time is ticking and there is a target on Sam's back . . .

ELLIOT LONG

SCAR COUNTY SHOWDOWN

Complete and Unabridged

LINFORD
Leicester

First published in Great Britain in 2011 by
Robert Hale Limited
London

First Linford Edition
published 2012
by arrangement with
Robert Hale Limited
London

British Library CIP Data

Long, Elliot.
  Scar county showdown. - -
(Linford western library)
1. Western stories.
2. Large type books.
I. Title II. Series
823.9'14–dc23

ISBN 978–1–4448–1131–5

Published by
F. A. Thorpe (Publishing)
Anstey, Leicestershire

Set by Words & Graphics Ltd.
Anstey, Leicestershire
Printed and bound in Great Britain by
T. J. International Ltd., Padstow, Cornwall

This book is printed on acid-free paper

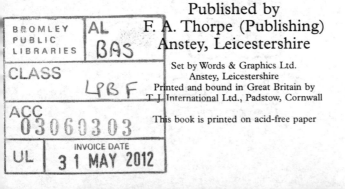

1

Around five o'clock that hot Monday afternoon Sam Curry rode into Columbus, the newly proposed county seat for Scar County now Hartville was considered unsuitable. He walked his tired roan up the busy Main Street, which at present was inches deep with dust as fine as well milled flour.

Ten, maybe fifteen miles to the north, across the flats beyond the town he observed the Sawbuck, Consolation and Lonesome mountain ranges. They were standing shoulder to shoulder like dark solemn giants against the pale sky before sweeping a wide arc toward the far, hazy east. After that they collapsed down into benchland that ended up as grasslands, undulating toward the south and west.

Sam was heading for City Hall, the impressive white-painted wooden building he'd heard so much about. It was built on the rise of ground at the eastern end of town. As he approached the edifice he decided it looked like one of those southern mansions the cotton planters used to build in their heyday. And Sam knew the story behind the construction. Grant Blake, the prominent New York entrepreneur, had it built. It was said Grant was on a visit to look over his mining interests. Before he returned east he declared his passion for hunting, preferably in mountain regions and alone. Thus informed, the manager of his two profitable mines dutifully organized a three-day hunt in the Consolations, though not for Grant to hunt alone. The manager made it clear he was not prepared to take that chance with so many wild Apaches still breaking out of San Carlos reservation and using the Consolations as an escape route to Mexico.

Needless to say, the hunt went well and it was claimed Grant fell in love with 'this big and beautiful country of yours'. He continued. 'And, John, I cannot wait to visit again'.

And Grant proved to be a man of his word. Every year in the fall he returned, carting his wife and three children with him. Carting because it was rumoured those unfortunates had to be dragged here kicking and screaming on account of their hatred of the place. Indeed, it was said his wife Clementine's opinion was that Columbus had no endearing features at all. All that could be found here were bugs, oafs, dust, death and profanity of the vilest kind. In fact, Clementine haughtily proclaimed, it was truly the most horrendous place it had ever been her misfortune to visit. Sam rubbed his bristled chin as he recalled the rest of the story. For, needless to say, something had to happen — a tenderfoot alone in wild, untamed country. And it did, in the fall of 1884. It was said Grant was dressed up in the most fashionable of hunting gear the East could offer when he had the misfortune to meet up with a bunch of marauding Chiricahua Apaches.

The Cherry Cows were making their way through the Consolations and the theory was they heard the boom of Grant's high-powered, scoped hunting rifle. Despite the urgency of their flight and the proximity of the sweat-oozing, cursing troopers not ten miles to their rear, the Cherry Cows still made time to deal with this corpulent, rosy-faced intruder upon their tribal homelands.

The result wasn't pretty. When the bluecoats came upon Grant's mutilated body the following day they said they had never seen the like of it, even with umpteen hard fought campaigns under their belts.

Naturally, the butchering of such a prominent figure made headline news nationwide. But the real surprise came when, months later, Grant's lawyers informed Columbus town's governing committee that Grant had left his sumptuous house to the town with no strings attached. All the family required was for a brass plaque to be placed in a prominent position on the building, announcing that Grant Blake was the generous benefactor. Needless to say, the committee pounced upon the offer and saw to it that that small requirement was honoured in full.

To round the whole thing off, Grant's eldest son, Sebastian, despite his known aversion to the town, made the long journey by train and coach here to Columbus especially to attend the solemn handing over ceremony and to personally view the plaque on behalf of all the family. It was one hell of a generous gift.

Jolting Sam out of his ruminations, two young females came out of the main door of City Hall gaily laughing and skipped down the steps leading from it holding hands. They were dressed alike in blue and white striped blouses, black ankle length skirts and broad-brimmed straw sun hats.

They came hurrying towards him.

Sam smiled and touched the rim of his border sombrero but they looked alarmed by the sight of him and gave him a wide berth as they bustled past. Sam was not greatly surprised by their reaction; he was well aware of the unease he could stir up in some people. To the casual onlooker, Sam Curry was a fearsome-looking *hombre*. He was six feet three inches tall with shoulders that suggested bull strength. He rode proud in the saddle and his grim, tanned face was made even more forbidding by the mask of alkali-loaded dust that, at the moment, caked it. Adding to that already formidable appearance was the white knife scar that ran from the top of his forehead, across his left eye, though not damaging it, to the left edge of his jaw — the line of which gave the impression it was formed out of a steel girder rather than mere bone. Without doubt, that terrible gash, rightly or wrongly, usually killed stone dead any suggestion a man or woman might have harboured regarding finding even a smidgen of warmth in Sam Curry. But those who knew Sam well would say that reaction was misplaced, even unkind, for Sam Curry could be as caring as the next man, if he was given the opportunity to demonstrate it. Yet, denying that opinion again, the cold impact of his blue stare, which at this moment was peering out from under his dusty sombrero and missing nothing, fully endorsed those daunting impressions. And not helping any, the ivory-handled Colt single-action sixgun, secured in the well oiled, tied-down holster at his right thigh, and the big Bowie knife sheathed across the small of his back, reinforced the overall effect. Without doubt, the reaction most people experienced when coming into contact with Sam Curry was: here was a man to walk very carefully around.

Reaching the four-horse tie rail before City Hall, Sam dismounted tiredly and tied up the sweat-streaked roan, loosening the girth to ease the horse's breathing. After that, while staring around, he stretched his lean frame by pushing his arms skywards and sawing them up and down while slowly gyrating his hips. Next he stamped his long, muscular legs and did a few knee bends to finish off the loosening up process. The kinks and aches in his back and legs now eased, he momentarily reflected on the end of his journey — the long, hard ride that brought him from his ranch on the banks of the San Luis, south of the border, to here, Columbus, Arizona Territory. Then he took in a deep breath, spat cotton into the dust and climbed the three broad white-painted wooden steps that took him up to the pillared gallery that ran the length of the building. After that, he entered City Hall's foyer through the large, wide-open and brass-hinged mahogany doors.

A small, balding, dark-suited man with gold-rimmed spectacles was putting on his coat behind the polished mahogany desk. He was facing the hall tree from which he had just lifted down his grey jacket. He had his back to Sam and without turning said, 'We're closed.' Still not looking he leaned back and pointed to the large, white-faced clock with the Roman numerals, situated high and flat against the wall he was facing. 'Five o'clock, on the dot; no more business done after that.'

Sam sighed, took off his sombrero and batted it against his thigh. Then he wiped his sweat-muddied brow with his handkerchief. Dust floated down from his hat on to the polished floorboards beneath his booted feet. He replaced his hat and handkerchief, glanced at the clock and said, 'Yup, five o'clock, on the button. Now, is Mayor Vincent Guthrie still here?'

'Like me he finishes at five. He won't see anybody now. You'll have to come back tomorrow.'

Sam said, 'He'll see me. Where's his office?'

The clerk turned, opened his mouth to deny the man but when he got a full view of him he saw there was something very threatening about him, something very deadly and he quickly changed his mind. He shrugged, pointed to the passage nearby and said, 'Room seven, but he won't like it.'

Sam said, 'He'll like it.'

He walked down the corridor, found number seven. The door was open. He tapped on the jamb and then walked in.

He stared at the burly, solidly built man, sitting head down behind the large oak desk. Vincent Guthrie was writing, making an entry into what appeared to be a ledger. Sam also saw Vince's curly hair was still fiery ginger, but now streaked with grey. A bald patch was also showing. It gave the impression Vince was wearing a tonsure. Top of that, Vince's bushy sideburns were almost grey, too.

Vince looked all business: the blue jacket of his suit was hooked over the back of his upholstered swivel chair; his embroidered flowery vest was fully unbuttoned and his light blue cravat was untied and laid over the back of his chair. His white, frilled silk shirt was open at the neck and the sleeves were rolled up to reveal thick arms that were matted with grey and ginger hair. Sam saw that globules of sweat were mottling Vince's forehead and shiny runnels of it were making slow tracks down his round, florid features.

Vince looked up with amber eyes when he heard Sam's tap. Seemingly approving of what he saw he smiled broadly, got up, closed the ledger and came around the desk. He extended his ham-like hand and grasped Sam's outstretched paw. He pumped it warmly and enthusiastically as he said, 'Sam Curry! By God, man, I did not expect you until tomorrow. You have made good time.'

Sam returned the shake firmly and said, 'I consider the news required it.'

Vince pumped his hand once more before releasing it. Then he stared hard at the scar on Sam's face. But instead of commenting on it right then he said, 'How long has it been? Ten years?'

'Almost to the day.' Sam looked around. 'For an ex-trail town lawman, Vince, you seem to have done pretty well for yourself.'

Vince shrugged modestly. 'I'm not complaining. I have mining interests — the OK mine in the Consolations and I have a thriving gaming palace, The Ace in the Hole, right there on Main Street.'

Sam nodded. 'I passed it on the way in. Real impressive.'

'I would say so,' Vince said without boast. Now he pursed his plump red lips. 'I guess I got lucky, found my true niche in life.'

Sam said, 'You always claimed a man made his own luck.'

Vince smiled indulgently. 'So I did, so I did.' He patted his belly and then pointed, his face quizzical, and said, 'If it's not an impertinent question, Sam . . . the scar on your face; how come?'

Sam touched the vivid wound self-consciously, but he did not mind his old friend's inquiry. However, he resolved only to say, 'It was a real close shave, I can tell you that.'

Vince's bushy, greying brows rose and amusement danced in his amber eyes. 'Some razor! The barber's dead, I take it?'

'I'm afraid so.'

Vince chuckled. 'Well, it figures. But, enough of this. How's Mexico, the *Hacienda San Luis*?'

'Passably pleasant.'

'Doing well?'

'No complaints.'

'Your wife, Consuelo, and the boy . . . OK?'

Sam said, with more enthusiasm now, 'Boy's got a little sister now, name of Elisa. Eighteen months old.'

'Wonderful!' Vince said and then screwed up his face in half-inquiry. 'But I never did quite figure out why you chose Mexico as a place to live.'

Sam pursed his lips. 'Being Mexican, Consuelo wanted it,' he said, 'but, end of the day, I got to like the idea as well.'

Sam's thin lips now tightened and his blue stare searched the face of his friend of former days, days when they were working as trail town lawmen up in Kansas. 'Vince,' he said, 'though I find this talk agreeable, I didn't come here to chat about my family — not right now, anyway. You know what I want to know: how did my brother Arthur die?'

Vince's face took on a sober look and he shook his head. 'It was a god-awful thing, Sam, no other way to describe it. Arthur was unarmed. He was playing billiards at Paddy Kirkpatrick's Billiards Parlour, that's on Second Street. It was as black as the inside of a bag out there that night. Arthur was bending over the table about to play the cannon that would've given him a fifty break, then, Bam! Bam! Two shots from beyond the street window.' Vince paused and sighed, his amber gaze engaging Sam's blue, arresting stare. 'He took both barrels in the back, Sam. God's truth, he did not deserve to die like that. He never stood a chance.'

The tired lines already etched into Sam's face, partly acquired after eight hot days in the saddle under a merciless sun, now deepened even more as he digested the news. 'Anyone arrested for it?' he said.

Vince shook his head. 'No. By the time folks in the room got over their shock and moved out to see what was going on, the killers had hoofed it.'

'Killers?' Sam said.

'Accomplices, more like,' Vince said. 'Only one did the actual shooting. A witness outside, using what lamplight there was, said he saw three men running away from the scene, but it was too dark to identify them. He claimed there was also a fourth man, waiting with the horses down by Marie Grafton's Gowns and Millinery on the corner of Third Street and Main.' Vince paused, staring searchingly into Sam's blue gaze as he added, 'They were all masked up, Sam. It was a planned, slick operation. They meant to kill Arthur and they got the job done.'

Sam tried to clear the sudden dryness in his throat with a 'harrumph'.

'Got it in the back, huh?' he said. He sighed. 'Well, that was the only way they could have nailed old Arthur.' His look was now searching. 'Have you got any ideas as to who could have done such a thing, Vince?'

'Sure I've got *ideas*,' Vince said, 'but it's a different matter to prove them, as well you know.'

Sam said, 'Even so, go on.'

Vince sighed. 'My guess is it was the Wright boys, John, James and Jeff, or four of their gang ordered to do it. The Wrights own the Blue Jay spread on Black Water Creek, fifteen miles southwest of here. They run mostly horses, but my guess is it's just a front for their more lawless activities.' Vince paused, shook his head. 'The Wrights are a bad lot, Sam. They can kill without regret and have connections with most of the rogue elements in the county. Chiefly, they do cross-border rustling, but lately they seem to have been branching out. It is suspected they were in on a payroll hold-up three weeks ago. The cash was destined for Durban Mining Ventures Ltd, one of several companies operating out there in the Sawbuck, Consolation and Lonesome mountain ranges to the north. Rumour has it they got away with more than twenty thousand dollars.' Vince sighed. 'Well, as you can imagine, the mine owners didn't like it and are now beginning to wonder what the hell they're paying taxes for.'

Sam scrubbed his bristled chin thoughtfully. 'That still don't explain why they killed Arthur, *if* they did. Being town marshal and responsible solely for things happening in town, where's the connection?'

Vince sighed again. 'That's easy. Arthur was prone to lean heavily on members of the Wright gang whenever they came into town. He just did not like crooks, I guess. And, Sam, I don't need to tell you, Arthur always wanted to be in the thick of things and he found it frustrating sitting here in town while all the action was going on out there.' Vince waved a hand toward the big windows, the view from which looked past the shady cottonwoods, east and toward the distant benchlands. He added, 'So he began to ride shotgun for the Gorman and Bailey stage line.'

Vince now opened the left hand top drawer of the desk and slid out a spring-loaded wrist holster with a twin barrelled Derringer clipped in it. He strapped it to his right arm.

Sam smiled when he saw it and said, 'Seems old habits die hard.'

Vince also grinned. 'This ain't Dodge City, but close enough to it.' He rolled down his shirtsleeves, fastened the gold cufflinks and buttoned up his shirt to the neck, then began tying his cravat using the mirror behind him.

While he was doing so Sam picked up on the previous conversation. 'Riding shotgun still ain't a reason to kill him.'

'Maybe you'll change your mind when you hear this,' Vince said. 'Arthur was riding guard on the stage carrying a payroll for the Good Times Mine. They were held up going through Manteca Pass, that's in the Consolations. Arthur being Arthur right off opened up with his Parker shotgun and killed Arkansas Jack Reed outright. Arkansas was a known rider with the Wright gang. Arthur also winged another of the three that were in on the hold-up. Well, that proved enough for them and the two still standing lit out.'

Sam said, 'Are you saying the Wrights were behind the hold up?'

Vince gestured with a large hand. 'Looked that way to me with Arkansas Jack Reed dead in the dust. However, all three men were masked and because of that, the two that rode away could not be positively identified. But Arthur wasn't through. You know what he was like. Because Arkansas Jack Reed was implicated he suspected the Wright gang and when they rode into town two days later, he challenged John Wright and Wild Man Haines about the hold up — Haines is John's right hand man these days, since old man Wright was killed while rustling beeves down Mexico way. In my reckoning that is their main occupation . . . bleeding Mexican ranchers white. However, they denied all knowledge of the hold up; claimed Arkansas Jack must have been acting on his own, maybe hiring two up-country *cabróns* to help him out. It certainly wasn't anything to do with the Blue Jay. They maintained they were not thieves but legitimate horse dealers. You know the kind of stuff those bastards come out with, Sam, as well as I do. What was more, they had the cheek to say they were sick and tired of being hounded every time they came into town and for Arthur to cut it out.' Vince sighed. 'Sam, they're goddamned liars! They were in on it all right.' Vince paused, his look earnest. 'They can lie real well, Sam, and the devil of it is the county sheriff, Mallory Grison, usually backs their stories. When he was called upon to give his opinion on the Manteca Pass job and to take action, he claimed he had already questioned the boys about the hold up the previous day, out there at the Blue Jay. He said they all had good alibis and came to the opinion it was like they claimed — Arkansas was acting on his own.'

'But you don't believe that,' Sam said.

'No, I don't.'

'So, are you saying the county law is siding with these cowboys?'

Vince said, 'Not *siding* exactly, nevertheless Grison doesn't bend over backwards to condemn them either. He claims they are being unjustly put on and sadly the local news rag, the *Scar County Clarion*, backs him up. I guess this is still predominantly cow country, Sam, but things are changing fast. Settlers have been coming in for two, three years now, claiming their 160 acres under the Homestead Act of 1862, the proviso being they pay their ten dollar deposit and work the land for five years.'

Sam rubbed his chin, 'hmmed' and nodded. 'Yes, I am aware of the Act and the conditions appertaining, and we both know from old that sodbusters and ranchers don't mix.'

'Well, they're having to learn how to and *pronto*,' Vince said. 'The sodbusters have government backing.'

Vince pulled on his gaudy vest, buttoned it and stuck a diamond pin into his cravat. Then he eased on his jacket. Fully dressed now and looking like *the* man about town he said, 'Sam, no matter what Haines and Wright claim, it is my opinion your brother's death was in revenge for killing Arkansas Jack Reed. Dammit, it's written all over it.'

Sam raised brows. He said, 'It seems that way.' He rubbed his chin. 'You said in your telegraph, after my inquiry regarding a law position, that a federal law badge was waiting for me, if or when I decided to cross the border.'

Vince nodded. 'That of deputy US marshal. Marshal Tim May, based in Hartville, personally cleared it with the territorial authorities three days ago and wired me, said he would send the badge up by courier. It arrived this morning. I guess they want to reinforce the local complement so they can keep the lid on things while the sodbusters and ranchers sort themselves out. At the moment Hartville is the county seat, but not for long is the strong rumour. The town is dying on its feet now the silver's run out and Columbus is being tipped as the town to replace it.'

Sam 'hmmed' and said, 'Mallory Grison, the Scar County sheriff you mentioned; is he likely to give trouble?'

'Well, he doesn't like your appointment,' Vince said. 'He thinks there is enough law hereabouts, what with his own squad of six deputies and the four town marshals that are spread throughout the county, as well as part-time constables.'

Vince looked in the mirror on the wall, straightened his jacket and put on his grey fedora hat, setting it at a rakish angle. Then he turned and said, 'Sam,

Grison bends over backwards to see the cowboys' side of things.' He offered a cynical grin. 'But I guess that's not surprising, seeing as the cowboys still hold the majority vote in the county.'

Sam nodded. Out of long experience, he knew how these things worked. He said, 'But for how long with the nesters coming in and miners already here. My guess is the mine owners will certainly be coaxing their men to vote differently, with their payrolls being stolen, and little being done about it.'

Vince raised ginger-grey brows. 'You guess right. But Grison does not seem to see that, or does not want to, and I suspect he'll try to forestall every effort he legally can to keep his popularity with the cowboys alive and this range free of homesteaders. That said, I think he is beginning to read the writing on the wall; he's politic enough for that.'

Sam said, 'Did he organize a posse when Arthur was murdered?'

'Sure he did,' Vince said, 'he's good at making gestures. Story has it the posse rode as far as Clay's Crossing — that's a widening in the road about fifteen miles out, in the hills east of here, by Ceremony Creek. The Wright crowd use it when they don't want to be bothered riding into Columbus. There are about a dozen tarpaper shacks there, and a well stocked liquor-and-goods store. Some Mexican adobes are huddled there, too. They've been there since God knows when.' Vince offered a cynical grin. 'Grison claimed it was getting dark by the time they arrived so they stayed the night. Any damned excuse, if you ask me.' Vince's amber stare now focused fully on Sam. 'Well, it goes without saying that, come morning, they were fit for nothing due to the likker they'd drank and the cards they'd played most of the night. Even so, they took up the search again, but not for long. They said the tracks petered out in the Saranoga badlands and it was pointless to go on.' Vince picked up his spectacle case and put it in his inside jacket pocket. 'Sam,' he added, 'I'm sure I don't have to tell you that posse consisted mostly of cowboys.'

Sam pursed his lips. 'Way it's sounding, the sooner I head for Hartville and take that US marshal's oath the better.'

Vince looked triumphant and waved the piece of paper, which had been lying on the large oak desk before him. 'No need for that, this here note gives me the authority to do that very thing, right here in this office.'

Sam felt as though a burden had been lifted from his shoulders. He did not fancy another long ride so soon after his journey up from Mexico. 'The hell it does. Well, dammit, let's get on with it.'

Vince recited the oath from the piece of paper and Sam accepted it. But then he put the badge into his pants pocket and said, 'Vince, I'd appreciate it if you would keep my appointment and who I am under your hat for now.'

His friend looked a little mystified

but he said, 'Sure, but why, Sam? Your fame as a successful lawman in the Kansas cattle towns, Hayes in particular, is well known. It stands to reason, with so many cowhands hereabouts, that some of them must have bumped into you one time or another up there and will recognize you, as they did me when I first arrived here. Grison knows who you are anyway; I had to tell him. He must have passed on the news.'

Sam sighed his resignation. 'Can't be any other way, I guess. Even so, I'd like to try it; circulate as a cowpoke looking for work for a while, see if I can pick anything up regarding Arthur's death. All cowboys can't be crooks. And while we're on it, have any of the homesteaders been bothered by the ranchers?'

Vince said, 'One has been burnt out, another has been dragged and died because of it; five have been intimidated badly enough to leave. Been no arrests, though — lack of evidence, is Grison's claim. All the raiders have been masked, he points out. Could be anybody, even neighbouring settlers with a grudge.' Vince's amber stare now had warning in it. 'Sam, circulating as a puncher will be a risky business and remember, you're a federal lawman now, here to deal with federal matters. Above all, Marshal May asked me to make it clear that you must not turn this into a personal vendetta. The investigation into Arthur's death must be conducted in accordance with federal rules.'

Sam levelled his blue gaze on to his old friend. He said, 'Vince, the moment Arthur was killed this became personal. Nevertheless, I'll do my job. However, meantime, if anything turns up pertaining to Arthur's death, I can give no promises as to what action I will take in that event.'

Vince's look was still serious. He said, 'All the same, *amigo*, there is a lot of politics involved here. One false step and Grison will come down on you like a ton of bricks and you can bet the *Scar County Clarion* will crucify you. That rag is fully cowboy orientated.'

Sam nodded, raised his brows and said, 'Welcome to Columbus.' He compressed his lips. 'Well, your concerns are noted, Vince. Now, one more question . . . has Arthur's post been filled?'

Vince stared, frowned. 'You mean that of town marshal?'

'Yes.'

'Not yet. Why?'

'I'd like my brother, Malachi, to take the job on.'

Vince's jaw dropped. '*Malachi*?'

'Yes,' Sam said. 'It seems to me we are going to need reinforcements and Malachi has pedigree. What's more, he's handy, Tucumnaco way to be exact. That's thirty miles across the Mex border in Sonora — horse-trading, he says. Tucumnaco even has a telegraph office with links across the border. Malachi could be here within a week if I wire him.'

Vince stared, his florid face full of doubt. '*Horse-trading*? Is that what he calls it?' He shook his head. 'Hell, I don't know, Sam. Malachi was always a touch erratic, in some cases dubious. It doesn't do these days. Dammit, why didn't you ask for the job yourself? It's more your style.'

'I would have,' Sam said, 'only I want to move around freely, ask questions and a US marshal's badge will give me authority to do that.'

Vince still looked to have several misgivings about putting forward Malachi Curry for the job of keeping the peace in Columbus. Nevertheless, he said, 'It can be arranged, I guess. But I'll be honest with you, Sam, I don't like it.'

'Too much family?'

'For one, yes, for another, the *Scar County Clarion* will make a meal out of it. Sam, you know Malachi's unconventional ideas about law enforcement as well as I do, as well as his penchant for rash gambling, not to say downright lawbreaking when it suits him.'

'You had a big yen for gambling

yourself one time, Vince,' Sam pointed out, 'it ain't a crime.'

'Not denying it,' Vince said, 'and I'm still in the business. But, believe me, that rag will exploit every opportunity if Malachi steps out of line.'

'Even so, can you swing his appointment?'

Vince said, 'Yes, but I'm not happy about it.'

Sam said, 'I'll have a word with him; try to put him straight on some points. He'll listen to me.'

Vince said, 'Yeah, but will he take any notice?' He held his hands out imploringly. 'Sam, as I have already pointed out, this is not just about your brother's death; it's about a whole raft of other things going on in this county. I made that clear in my telegram. But if you do catch and kill the bastards that bushwhacked Arthur, well, the governor says he will have few hang ups about how it was done and will deal with any kick-backs there might be regarding it. Arthur was well liked. Even so, people will need to know that all lawlessness is being dealt with, and not just you and your brother's need for revenge. I hope you appreciate that.'

Sam said, 'Vince, we've been friends a long time, stared through a lot of gunsmoke together, done a lot of law enforcement together, along with Arthur and occasionally Malachi. However, you are out of that now, what with your business commitments and your mayoral responsibilities. Let me worry about the law and its administration, OK? I swear I will play it down the line.' He stuck out his hand. 'Do we have a deal?'

Vince hesitated and then smiled and took the offered hand and said, 'I guess we have a deal.'

Sam grinned along with him though the scar down his face made it into more of a leer. 'Looks like I've ridden slap bang into a hornet's nest here, Vince.'

His friend released his hand and said, 'Damn right you have, and it won't be pretty if or when the lid comes off.'

Sam's blue stare became intense, hard as sapphire. 'Arthur's killer will be brought to justice, Vince, no matter what. But I'll do my best to help clean up Scar County on the way.'

Vince's stare was equally as frank. He said, 'Sam, I've really stuck my neck out on this. Don't let me down.'

Sam laid a hand on his friend's arm. 'Vince, we go back a long way. You know me better than that.'

'Yeah, guess I do.'

Sam said, 'Now, one last thing . . . where is Arthur's grave?'

Vince was straightening up a few papers on the desk and putting them in one of the desk drawers. Clearly he was preparing to leave. 'No problem,' he said. He lifted out his pocket watch and added, 'I have a few minutes to spare. I'll take you to it if you like.'

Sam felt warmth for his old friend rise up in him once more. 'Well, I appreciate that, Vince, I really do, but first I want to see to my horse and find lodgings. Just tell me where I can find the grave. That will do.'

'Back of the only church we got,' Vince said. 'Just ask anybody.' He added, 'I gave him a real fine send off, Sam, just like you would have wanted.' Enthusiasm now lit up Vince's amber stare. 'By God, Sam . . . me, you, Arthur and Malachi — we made a great town-taming team during those Kansas trail town days, didn't we? It still stirs my blood to think about them.'

Again Sam felt warmth for his friend. 'Still got the yearn, huh?'

Sam felt Vince grip his arm and squeeze it gently. 'I'll see you around, compadre. Got to rush.'

Sam nodded. 'Sure, fellow.'

Vince now patted Sam's shoulder affectionately and then hurried away.

By the time Sam reached the end of the passageway and was entering the foyer, Vince was going through the big open doors. Moments later his friend was skipping down the gallery steps and heading for the centre of town, his squat, blocky frame earnestly and purposely leaning forward as he walked.

Sam shook his head at his old friend's haste. Dammit, Vince had been in a hurry ever since that first day he had sided him on the streets of Abilene, before law enforcing in Hayes became a major part of both their lives. Thinking on it, Vince's declared vow, even then, was to make it rich one day, despite his penchant for gambling big sometimes. Sam raised his brows. Well, it seems Vince had finally achieved his ambition and had nailed down that occasional rashness at the gaming tables. Good luck to him. If ever a man had earned his success, Vince had.

2

Leaving City Hall Sam retightened the
girth and climbed up on to his tired
roan. The gelding needed feeding,
grooming and stalling after the long,
gruelling ride. Columbus was a big
town and Sam soon found a place to
leave his horse — Brown's Hay and
Grain on Third Street, Stalling Provided. It was not a very large place, but
Sam observed the stalls were clean and
the horses in them appeared to be well
cared for.

He dismounted just inside the big
doorway, at the edge of the long, gloomy,
straw-littered, but clean, runway. The
owner, Edward Brown, with a wooden
leg and cantankerous disposition by the
look on his grizzled face, came out of a
small box-like office just to the right of
the big doors.

Brown eyed him up and down with

rheumy grey eyes before he took the roan by the bridle and said, 'Stabling is a dollar a night, mister; grain twenty-five cents a half bucket, grooming will be thrown in with the straw bedding and feed hay. However, if you're planning on staying a while, well, I can come down a tad on stabling. The rest stays the same.'

Sam said, 'I am planning on staying a while.'

Brown instantly grinned, revealing broken and tobacco-stained teeth. 'Then you got yourself a deal. Now, what was your name again? Mine's Ed Brown.'

Despite Vince's reservations back at City Hall about what little use it would be, Sam found he still wished to stick to his plan of keeping his real name quiet for a spell. Why, he wasn't sure, because Vince's argument that he was once a renowned trail-town lawman and that he was in the middle of range country, with probably half the riding population hereabouts having visited those Kansas hellholes at one time or another, meant he was bound to be recognized. However, he had thought the matter over on the ride to Ed Brown's and was still minded to believe it would be a good idea to do so. Then one of his rare bouts of idiosyncrasy cut in. He said, 'How about Ulysses S Grant?'

Brown's eyes rounded in disbelief. 'You've got to be kidding me, mister.'

Sam shrugged. 'Take it or leave it.'

Ed Brown said, 'I'll take it, but, as to anybody else doing so, I figure they won't be so accommodating.' Then the old timer threw back his head and cackled a raucous laugh before he added, 'Ulysses S Grant, for Chris'sake!'

Beginning to like Ed Brown, which was an unusual event being of a cautious nature until pedigree was proved, Sam said, 'You find that crazy, huh?'

'I sure do,' Brown said, 'about as crazy as they come.' But then he screwed up his grey-bristled face in inquiry and leaned forward. 'You got a place to stay yet, *Ulysses?*'

Brown's emphasis on the name was not lost on Sam. He said, 'No, but I've got the feeling you're about to make a suggestion. Am I right?'

Brown grinned. 'Mary Summerbee's place west of town, right at the end of Fourth Street,' he said. 'It's a mighty handsome rooming house, the prices are reasonable and it's in a quiet situation.'

'A relative of yours?' Sam said.

Brown looked offended. 'No, dammit, she's just a nice immigrant lady down on her luck and trying to make an honest living. Something wrong with that?'

'Nothing at all,' Sam said, raising his hands. 'Saddle and things be safe here?'

Brown now looked resentful. 'Sure they will! Hang what you're leaving on the stall wall and I'll deal with it.'

Sam smiled his scar-deformed smile and said, 'Fair enough, old timer.'

He drew his Winchester out of its saddle boot and untied his calfskin suitcase with the changes of clothing Consuelo had placed in it before he left

Hacienda San Luis. Then he peeled off dollars from his roll and placed them in Ed Brown's gnarled right hand. Brown counted the notes and then grinned his brown-toothed grin. 'Seems you mean what you say, mister — 'bout staying a while.'

Sam pointed a finger. 'Got it in one, old timer. *Adios.*'

'*Adios* yourself . . . *Ulysses.*' Ed cackled another laugh, again clearly enjoying the emphasis he put upon the word.

Sam was going out through the big swing doors when the noise of three rapidly fired rifle shots tore the approaching evening quiet of Columbus town apart. And then all hell broke loose. The sudden din sent the six mules pulling the passing wagonload of miners, presumably in for a night on the town, into a wild gallop up this narrow back street. The driver was already howling furious expletives. Pedestrians and riders also using the thoroughfare ran for cover, startled anxiety on their features. The horses in the stalls behind Sam became restless, too; one or two were kicking at the stout walls in their alarm.

And it was within the compass of that extended instant that Sam became aware of two pieces of lead, ripping bright chunks of timber out of the board door not an inch from his head and a third bullet ricocheting off the iron door hinge. That hunk of refined galena went buzzing like a hornet up through the roof of Ed Brown's stabling facility. Almost immediately dust and debris began showering down, their particles shining like gold dust in the late afternoon rays of the sun, slanting in through the big stable doors.

'Holy cow!' Ed howled.

'Get under cover, old timer!'

Sam dropped to the ground, his heart already pumping hard. He let go of his suitcase and rolled to the cover of the nearest wall. As soon as he was into its refuge he got to his feet and jacked a round into the breech of his Winchester. Now peering through a chink in the wallboards, he quickly weighed up the situation outside.

The back street was now deserted of traffic and pedestrians. Drifting in the maw of the alley opposite, with the Assay Office forming a corner of it, Sam saw blue tendrils of gunsmoke drifting on the hot, near-still air. Without hesitation, he ran out through the doors jacking off four shots into the alley's opening before completing a zigzag path across the street.

His shoulder coming up hard against the assay office wall he pressed against its warm boards and waited, his breathing rasping, his nerves taut as newly strung fence wire. But what was really surprising him was his body: it was quivering like a jelly and his throat was as dry as the Sonora desert. This reaction to danger dismayed him. Ten years of comparatively easy living at the *Hacienda San Luis* — apart from the incident in which that drunken *vaquero* put this scar on his face — must have made him a tad soft. He needed to rectify that.

Tightening his resolve, he peered round the edge of the office building. He did not know what to expect. To his relief he found the alley was deserted, tranquil even, in the yellow light of this late afternoon sun. It was then he heard hoof beats at the top of the backstreet, off to his left — the bushwhacker making his escape?

Steeling himself, because he wasn't altogether sure, Sam stepped out pulling his rifle to his shoulder. He sighted it, ready to shoot at an instant's notice for he estimated he would only have a second or two to get off effective shots. The horseman appeared, firing his Colt at Sam as he crossed the head of the narrow street.

Ignoring the lead hissing past him Sam jacked off two shots. But already the building at the top end of this backstreet was hiding the rider and Sam saw his lead harmlessly ripping chunks out of the woodwork.

Silently fuming, Sam released his breath. He lowered his rifle and glared at the space that was now filled only with his own gunsmoke.

At that moment Ed Brown came running awkwardly across the street, hindered by his wooden leg. He was carrying a twin-barrelled Wells Fargo shotgun in his right hand, Sam's calfskin bag in his left.

When the oldster got close, Sam stared at the potentially devastating weapon in the oldster's work-gnarled right hand. He said, 'Were you planning on using that shotgun, old timer?'

Brown said, 'If I had to.'

'Birdshot or buckshot?' Sam said.

'Buck.' Brown leered his broken-toothed grin with the three gaps in it. 'I guess somebody knows who you really are, huh?' he said. 'And, sure as hell, it ain't Ulysses S Grant. Now the cat's out of the bag, I'd say it was Sam Curry. Am I right?'

Sam stared at the oldster before he

allowed his grimace of a smile to spread across his deformed lips. 'You knew my name all along, huh?'

Ed Brown spat brown juice and nodded. 'Pushed beeves into Hayes a couple of times when I was riding for the Double Bar M, a south Texas brand. That was before I got my leg busted and cut off below the knee 'cause of gangrene. Mister, I ain't likely to forget your face, you pulled me out of a real bad jam one night, though your mug has got more than a wee bit messed up since I last saw it.'

Sam self-consciously touched his scar; his facial lines setting into hard lines. He said, 'There were lots of incidents and lots of faces in those days, Ed, yours was just one of them.'

Brown nodded. 'I reckon so. You going to Mary Summerbee's now?' He pointed up the back street hopefully. 'Fourth Street's thataway, two blocks up.'

'Any bugs?' Curry said.

Ed Brown looked aghast and his grey

brows shot up. 'Cleanest damned place in the whole of town,' he said, 'and you can kick my ass if you find it ain't.'

Curry smiled, despite his now growing tiredness. It had been a long, hard eight days on some really treacherous mountain trails. However, he said, 'That's a real rash statement to make, old timer, and I might hold you to it. But thanks for coming to give a hand just now. It don't happen very often.'

'Least I could do,' Brown said. Then he sniffed and squinted, his old face becoming intensely curious. 'You come to see into your brother's death, ain't you.' Ed made it a statement.

Sam said, 'You've guessed it.'

Brown sniffed again. 'You taking over his job?'

Sam offered another distorted grin. He said, 'You're asking too many questions, old man.'

Brown returned the smile. 'I'll take that as a yes.'

Sam said, 'You're getting close, but not quite. *Adios, anciano.*'

Brown said, 'It's got to be federal lawing, then.'

Sam prepared to walk away. 'Read it how you will.'

Brown nodded, his look gleeful. 'Already done it.' Then he waved the calfskin bag in the air. 'Afore you go, how about this?'

Sam smiled his ugly smile. 'You know, old timer, with all this excitement, I plum forgot it.'

He took the bag off the stable owner and said his goodbyes then strode off up the street, which was now becoming alive again with people and traffic after the past potentially murderous few minutes.

3

At the furthest end of the quiet Fourth Street Sam came to the board stuck in the lawn of a well tended garden with colourful flowers in it. It fronted a large, white-painted two-storey building. A gallery stretched the full length of the structure, and a blue, canopied swing settee was tucked in the far right corner. It was drifting lazily back and forth in the breeze that was coming in from the flat country beyond the town and was squeaking monotonously. Sam observed the board in the lawn announcing that this was Mary Summerbee's Rooming House. Good Food, Clean Sheets, A Friendly Welcome To All Decent Folk.

He hefted the still-warm long gun in his hand then went through the wicket gate and strolled up the short path and up the two steps and across the stoop to the closed fly door. The main door beyond was wide open. There was the smell of roast meat in the air and cooking vegetables, the aroma of apricot pie in the background.

His stomach rumbled, clearly craving a belly full of that good old home cooking for, truth be told, he had not eaten since daybreak. And that meal was only what was left of a large sidewinder he'd shot the previous day and cooked and ate the most of for supper the previous night.

He gently rapped the butt of his rifle on the door-jamb. Soon, a female shout came from inside, 'Go see whom that be, Jane.'

Sam soon saw a girl — she could be around ten years of age — come hustling down the passageway, her blue gingham skirts, under her white apron, rustling. She came out of the open door at the end of the hallway. When she got to the fly door she opened it. She had a round, and at that moment, heat-reddened face. A wealth of blonde, sweat-dampened curly hair topped her flushed countenance. Her solemn blue eyes gazed up into his. Surprisingly, the scar down his face did not seem to bother her. She said, 'Yes?'

'Looking for a room, little lady.'

She looked him up and down. She did not appear impressed. She said, 'Come in and sit in the hall, please. I've got to close the door. The flies. Mama will be with you in a minute or two.'

Sam said, 'Thank you kindly.'

He took off his sombrero, entered the hallway and sat down in one of the two chairs placed there. The butt of his Winchester clumped too noisily on to the polished floorboards, but the girl did not seem to notice as she closed the fly door and hurried past him, throwing him another curious glance. Before she went back to where she came from she paused by what Sam figured was the dining room door, a couple of yards up from where he was sitting. She shouted, 'Customer,' and then carried on into what Sam assumed was the kitchen. Presently a small, but well shaped woman, around twenty seven years of age, he guessed, and dressed in a severe black dress, came out of what he had already decided was the dining room. She turned grey eyes on to him and said, 'Won't keep you long, sir.'

She hustled off toward the kitchen, her black skirts rustling. After some moments she returned with a king-size tray upon which were two large tureens, one brimmed full of boiled potatoes the other loaded with vegetables. They looked too heavy for a woman of such slight build to be carrying, but carrying them she was and apparently without too much discomfort. The girl followed close behind with the huge roast resting on a large platter. It looked like beef.

Again Sam's stomach started to protest for, to him, after eight days of trail grub . . . bacon and beans and coffee mainly — rattlesnake the last day — this food smelt like something that had come down from heaven and he instantly decided this was the place for him.

Both females trooped into the dining room and soon compliments were coming thick and fast from the diners. After several moments the woman emerged, calling over her shoulder as she did, 'Get Mr Travers to carve and serve the joint, Jane, while you collect the soup dishes and return them to the kitchen. But tut, tut, girl, you know what to do without me having to tell you, so get on with it.' Then whom Sam took to be Mary Summerbee was before him. She was blowing a damp wisp of blonde hair out of her eyes. She was a grown up version of the girl, apart from the eyes, which were grey, not blue. Sam saw globules of sweat stippled her round, freckled and rather plain face; she was clearly hot and not a little flustered. Her appraisal of him was fulsome and thorough, particularly the ugly scar, but she was apparently not unduly disturbed by what she saw.

She said, 'Now, sir, be ye looking for

a room?' She had an English accent, with a soft pleasing burr to it.

He said, 'Yes, ma'am; Ed Brown recommended you.'

'Ha, Edward! That be nice of him. We have a room. How long will it be for?'

Sam pursed his scarred lips. 'Can't say exactly. Could be some time.'

'That be all right, sir,' she said, 'I'll take ye up to view it.'

Gathering his rifle and his calfskin bag Sam followed her upstairs. She discussed the charge per day, or per week on the way up and he was satisfied. More so when he found the room was clean, airy and looked out on to Fourth Street, which was standing quiet and serene in the rose-pink evening light.

'It be suitable, sir?' she said.

'No complaints at all, ma'am,' he said. He added, 'I'd like to wash up. I've been on the trail more than a week now.'

She pointed to the porcelain jug and

bowl on the washstand. She said, 'Ye can use that, sir, or ye can put your head under the yard pump outside, at the back. We have bath facilities but there be no hot water at the moment. I need notice.'

'The yard pump will do fine,' Sam said.

'That be settled then,' she said. 'Now, what be your name, sir?'

'Curry, Sam Curry.'

'Mr Curry,' she said. 'Be you hungry?'

'Yes.'

'Then I'll save ye some supper. Be that all right?'

'Fine with me, ma'am, and thank you, I wasn't expecting it.'

'No thanks be needed, sir. You are our guest now.'

She bustled off and Sam watched her go down the landing. He was already beginning to feel at home and it was a good feeling.

★ ★ ★

Stripped to the waist, Sam ducked under the yard pump. He sluiced his upper body with welcome ice-cold water then he dried himself with the towel Mary Summerbee had provided. After that he opened his cut-throat razor, lathered his face and shaved by touch. Satisfied he had done a reasonable job, even though he needed to use the cold water to shave, he swilled his face again and patted it dry. Then he returned to his room, reopened his calfskin bag and changed into the clean clothes and socks Consuelo had packed for him.

Pleased with his appearance, he went downstairs. Mary Summerbee met him at the bottom, smiling. She looked cool now, her skin a clear and healthy pink. She said, 'Do ye mind eating in the kitchen, Mr Curry? The dining room is made over to the parlour now.'

'No, ma'am, anywhere will do.'

'Well, that be fine. Now, please come through.'

The kitchen was spotless. The girl, Jane, and another woman were washing up the supper crocks at the big sink. Mary Brown waved him into a seat drawn up to the long, scrubbed-white deal table. Soon she laid beef and vegetables before him on a large plate. 'Eat up, Mr Curry,' she said, 'do not stand on ceremony. But sorry to say, the soup be finished.'

'That's no problem, ma'am,' Sam said. 'I wasn't expecting to be fed anyway, booking so late in the day.'

Mary Brown smiled in a matronly way. 'We aim to please, sir.'

'And you've done that in bucketfuls, ma'am.'

Sam found the meal was good and the apricot pie to follow was even better. Finally pushing his empty dessert dish aside he said, 'A mighty fine meal, ma'am, if I may say so.'

'You may,' Mary Summerbee said. 'Now, Mr Curry, breakfast be at seven, lunch be one after the noon hour, and supper be prompt at six of the clock in the evening. Be that satisfactory to you?'

'More than satisfactory, ma'am.'

Sam dabbed his lips with the serviette laid by the side of his plate. As he rose from the table Mary Summerbee said, 'If you be out and need to miss a meal I would appreciate you telling me, sir. Perhaps I can fix ye some food for the journey, if that is what you will be doing.'

'I'll remember that, ma'am, and thank you.'

Mary Summerbee smiled her plump-faced smile. 'That be fine then, sir. You may smoke in the dining room if you so wish. It doubles up as the lounge.'

Curry said, 'I smoke strong Sonoran *cigarillos*, ma'am, when I feel the urge, so I will use the balcony.'

Mary Summerbee looked at him with pleased grey eyes. 'Ye be a fine, considerate man, sir, and I will remember that courtesy. Now, if you don't mind me asking: be ye any relation to Marshal Curry?'

Sam said, 'He was my brother.'

'I see, so I be in order to offer my

condolences then?' She shook her head. ''Twas a terrible thing that happened, sir; Marshal Curry was a fine, fine man. He is badly missed in the town.'

Sam said, 'Thank you for your sentiments, Mrs Summerbee. Now, I will use your veranda, if I may?'

But Mary Summerbee was not finished. 'Rumour has it the cowboys did that frightful thing.'

'That is the story I've heard, too, ma'am.'

'But you do not trust that story?' Sam decided the woman had keen intuition.

He said, 'Not entirely, ma'am; I like to check things out for myself.'

'That be understandable,' Mary Summerbee said. 'Now, would ye be liking to meet the other guests before ye take tobacco?'

Sam decided such a thing could be useful. He said, 'I'd be happy to, ma'am.'

Entering the parlour/dining room he found it was surprisingly large. The table, he noticed, was now covered with a heavy red and gold cloth. The white tablecloth, he presumed, must be put away until the next meal, or removed for washing later. The dining chairs were now against the walls and six comfortable-looking armchairs were spread around. Soon as he entered the room six heads lifted from newspapers and books and eyes of different hues surveyed him keenly.

'Gentlemen, this be Mr Curry,' Mary Summerbee said.

Sam nodded, eyed up the occupants and said, 'Gents.'

A brisk moving, grey suited man rose immediately upon his entrance. He had bushy black hair, black wiry sideburns and a thick moustache. His brown eyes were clear and lively and his face was healthily tanned. He offered a calloused hand and Sam took it. The stranger said, 'Simon Graves, sir, manager of the Denson and Collins Mine, out there in the Sawbucks.'

Sam shook his hand once and firmly,

then released it. He said, 'Mr Graves.'

A thin, elegant looking man in a dark suit and grey cravat with a ruby pin stuck in it rose next. He had pale, thin features and clean, even teeth. He said, 'Ah am Jim Travers, ah deal cards at the Ace in the Hole.'

Curry shook his hand. 'Vince Guthrie's place?'

There was instant interest in Travers's eyes. 'You know Vincent, suh?'

'Yes; a friend I value.'

'Ah see. Well, suh, if it is not a presumption, are you any relation to Arthur Curry?'

'My brother.'

Travers raised brows. 'Ah find that interesting.'

Of the other four men two were drummers, one in whiskey, one in ladies' attire; the fifth man was another mine manager. The last to shake his hand gave his name as Tom Lacy. He was a burly, tanned, tough looking rancher wearing a smart brown town suit and tooled high boots. He narrowed his eyelids and leaned forward and said, 'Sam Curry, the Kansas town tamer, am I right?'

Sam said, 'That was a long time ago, Lacy, and I didn't tame, I kept the peace. There is a difference.'

'Even so, your name is remembered, and not always with favour, like it or not,' Lacy said. 'How come the scar?'

Sam fingered the vivid wound down his face. He was more than a little angered by the brusque reference to it and the unusual invasion of his privacy . . . not a common thing in these Western lands. 'My business, mister,' he said.

Lacy said, apparently without prejudice, 'Yeah, I reckon so. Well, I own the Double Six, out on the Rio Poco. The name's deceptive by the way because that river isn't small running at all. When it rains it can be a real bitch.' Lacy frowned now and narrowed his eyelids. 'You've come about your brother's murder?'

'That's the general idea.'

Lacy said, as if proud of his

perception, 'Yeah, figured it right away. You still toting a badge, Curry?'

Sam decided diplomacy was not one of Lacy's strong points. He looked around the assembly, one man at a time. 'Well, you might as well know, gents, I am now Deputy US Marshal Sam Curry, sworn in not two hours ago. Chiefly, I'm here to look into the murder of my brother. My other mandate is to look into the general situation prevailing on this range and help do something about it.'

'Knew it!' Lacy said with some triumph. 'Once a lawman, always a lawman.'

Growing a little tired of Lacy Sam said, his voice brittle, 'Come to think on it, what's your view on the present state of affairs in this county, Lacy, you being a rancher and all?'

Lacy lost his smile and said, 'Sodbusters, you mean? Well, hell, I'd as soon have them somewhere else.'

Sam said, 'From what I heard they're here to stay.'

Lacy's face set into pugnacious lines. 'Damn interfering government, sitting there in Washington God knows how many miles away. They don't know what they're doing, sending in such trash to our land.'

Sam said, 'You own your place?'

Lacy glared. 'I fought for that land, mister. And, sure as hell, nobody is going to take it from me.' Lacy looked around the room. 'I'm going for a drink. Any of you boys coming?'

Bill George, one of the mine managers, Isaiah Finkelstein, the whiskey drummer, and Jim Travers, the gambler, got up. George said, 'I'm your man, Lacy.' Finkelstein, the drummer, backed him up cheerfully. 'Count me in.' And Jim Travers looked at Sam and smiled. 'It's back to work for me, ah guess.' Sam held up his hand and stared at the Double Six rancher. 'Before you go, Lacy, what's your view on the people down on Black Water Creek?'

Lacy frowned. 'You mean the Wright boys, Wild Man Haines?'

'The same.'

Lacy said, 'The hell you mean, *my view?*'

Sam spread his palms. 'On the cross border rustling that's going on, the stage hold-ups; rumour has it those boys are in it up to their necks.'

Lacy's grey stare turned steely. He studied Sam for some moments before he said, 'I suggest you ask *them* that question, Deputy, not me.' He turned to the waiting men. 'Let's go, boys. Time's a wasting.'

But Sam's accusations set up a talking point as the men went out into the late evening. As Sam watched them depart, a hint of humour came to his blue gaze, but there was no suggestion that humour was going to reach his grim features. He wanted the man that murdered Arthur, wanted him with a burning passion, and he did not give a damn whose corns he trampled on in pursuit of that goal.

He went to the kitchen. Mary Summerbee was sitting at the scrubbed table, reading what looked like a well thumbed eastern magazine for ladies. The other woman was nowhere to be seen and Sam presumed the girl had gone to bed. Maybe the woman was the day help and lived in town.

Mary Summerbee looked up as he entered. She said, 'Be there something you need, Mr Curry?'

'The church, ma'am, where is it?'

Mary Summerbee's look was long and deep. 'Ah, yes, I take it ye will be wanting to view your brother's grave? And 'tis fortunate. I be planning to go that way myself, so I'll be getting my coat.'

Sam held up a calloused right hand. 'I don't want to put you to any trouble, ma'am. Directions will be enough.'

But Mary Summerbee was already pulling on her black overcoat, which had been draped over the back of one of the four chairs grouped around the table. Pulling on her black poke bonnet and tucking in her hair she said, 'No trouble, I go every night. You see, my husband is buried there, Mr Curry. I like a few quiet moments with him when I can find the time.'

Sam nodded. 'Clearly somebody dear to your heart, ma'am.'

Mary Summerbee's eyes dropped slightly. He saw the pain in them. She whispered, 'Yes, somebody very dear, Mr Curry.'

He followed her outside into the late evening light. He walked with her up Fourth Street. At its head they walked out toward the edge of town. They soon came to the church, a large frame building with a bell suspended in a tower, similar in style to the Mexican adobe bell towers, though this one was made of timber. It looked a recent build. Sam now saw there was a large plot cleared of scrub and weeds at the back of the building; a number of wooden headboards were already set into the stony soil. Mary Summerbee led him to the one that looked to be the newest of them. 'Here be your brother's last resting place, Mr Curry,' she said. 'The burial and the headboard was paid for by public subscription, organized by the mayor. Believe me, sir, when I say your brother was a much respected man hereabouts and is greatly missed in Columbus.'

Sam bobbed his head slightly. He said, 'I can only thank you again for your sentiments, ma'am; it is truly nice to know.'

'It be my pleasure, sir.'

Mary Summerbee's face, usually pale, was like pink alabaster in the rosy light of the setting sun. As if a little embarrassed by her last words she fumbled with her black poke bonnet and then straightened her black dress before she went on, 'Well, I'll leave ye to your mourning, sir.'

Sam said, 'You have been more than kind, Mrs Summerbee.'

'Be no trouble, sir.'

As Mary Summerbee departed Sam looked down. The headstone read: *Arthur Curry, respected marshal of this* town. *Died 16th August 1888. Foully murdered by persons unknown.*

Bitter resolve settled in the pit of Sam's stomach. Not unknown for long, he thought. Then he knelt and prayed.

4

Early the following morning Sam telegraphed Malachi. The answer came back three hours later — a typical Malachi exaggeration: he was already on his way. Meanwhile, waiting for Malachi to arrive, Sam rode the country around Columbus, to familiarize himself with the lay of the land. He called in on the homesteaders first and then some of the ranchers. Unsurprisingly, there were the usual complaints and aggressive talk from both sides. He listened but said little; he had heard it all before in other places, when keeping the peace was his regular occupation.

He passed several noisy mines in the mountains, three crashing stamp mills. For sure, the silver industry appeared to be booming. But best of all, nobody attempted to take a shot at him after that hair-raising incident in town. Some maverick cowboy with a grudge and a long memory? It was more than likely.

Tuesday of the second week, Malachi rode into town. Sam greeted him warmly. It was easy to tell they were brothers. The same brown hair, the same ever watchful blue stare, the same wide shoulders that tapered to narrow hips; the same chiselled features, except for the ugly scar on Sam's face. It could be said, even before Sam's face became so badly disfigured, that Malachi's features were the more agreeable-looking of the two. And there was often a devil-may-care look in his eyes where Sam's looks remained dour, brooding and thoughtful except when he was crossed; then they could become frighteningly hostile. Another feature that was absent on Sam's face was Malachi's pride and joy — his large walrus moustache. And Sam knew their mental attitudes differed markedly as well. Malachi could be erratic; he could allow his temper to get the better of him and often did, causing him to do things he often later regretted. And it was well known Malachi was deadly with the Smith & Wesson double-action he carried, holstered in the cross-draw position on his left hip. Unlike Sam, using that piece was never a last resort with Malachi, more like the first requirement saving a lot of time wasting later if the offender came back seeking revenge for his earlier humiliation. Top of that it was often said Malachi smiled as he faced up to a man on the prod, that he appeared to enjoy the high tension of the duel, the split-second blur between life and death that the drawing of weapons — with the brutal intention to kill — brought. On the other hand, Sam did not remotely find any pleasure in killing. Indeed, gunplay was always a last resort for him, even in the most dangerous of situations. Laying a Colt barrel across some hell-raising cowboy's head and throwing him into jail until he cooled off, then fining him ten dollars for his misdemeanours, had always been more his style. However, these were not the old days, Sam reminded himself. Now Sam Curry was hunting the killer of his brother and that was entirely another matter.

Brotherly greetings over, Malachi stabled his big strawberry roan mare at Ed Brown's place and then found lodgings up town at Sadie Thompson's establishment, Mary Summerbee's lodging house being full. After that, together they visited their brother Arthur's grave. Half an hour after noon, in the marshal's office there on Main Street, Vince Guthrie swore in Malachi and handed over the town marshal's badge, the badge Arthur had worn so proudly and effectively until the day of his murder.

Malachi stared at the tin star he held in the palm of his big right hand, turning it over and over before pinning it on. Then he said, more to himself, 'Here we are, Arthur, Sam and me. Be sure we'll put that murdering son of a bitch where he belongs — six feet under.' Then he pinned on the badge, looked up and grinned, first at Vince and then at Sam. 'Now, who's for some cards?' he said. 'Bar owning ten dollars, I'm fresh out of dinero. Got to beef up my bank roll.'

Sam recalled, as well as his unpredictability, there was this other thing with Malachi — his gambling. Admittedly, most men liked to shuffle the paste-boards, but it was near an obsession with Malachi. It was certainly a way of making extra money, because he was so good at it. Some would say, and did on occasion, that he was too good, but usually under their breath. However, some card men with stomach occasionally took exception to his uncanny luck, downright distrusted it even and called him out. Most got buried on Boot Hill. Needless to say, such a clinical end to those disputes did not help with Malachi's public image. Nevertheless, he remained an effective lawman, a man to have at your back. And despite his intermittent murderous inclinations when challenged, oddly, he also had this engaging personality. Indeed, some people found it infectious, even downright irresistible on occasion.

'Count me out,' Sam said.

'Me too,' Vince Guthrie said. 'I got business to attend to. Maybe later. It's about time I skinned *you*, for a change.'

Malachi looked disappointed. 'Goddamn, just wanting to get reacquainted, that's all. It's been a number of years since we were in the law business together, up there on those Kansas plains.'

Vince Guthrie was opening his mouth to voice a reply when the whiplash cracks of a discharging rifle echoed across the heat-swamped town — once, twice, three times — drowning out his words. Moments later the noon stage from Hartville careered past the grimy windows of the law office.

All three sets of eyes followed the clouds of dust it threw up in its wake. Walkers and riders alike were forced to scurry out of its way as it whirled past them on its way to Gorman and Bailey's waiting room, which doubled up as the town's post office, a hundred yards up Main Street.

Vince Guthrie, his florid face now tight and grave, switched his gaze on to Sam, then back to Malachi. He said, 'Now . . . that's got to be trouble, boys.'

No answer was needed. They went out of the marshal's office and paced up the street toward the stage depot. Approaching it, Sam saw the stage was pulled up in front of the office and the clearly shaken passengers were already disembarking. Two ladies and three men composed the complement of five travellers. Sam saw that the ladies were clearly distressed. They were being assisted across the street to the Rosalie Hotel and Dining Rooms.

Solomon Pierson the driver — Sam picked up his name after contact the previous week — was climbing down using one hand. Sam could see Sol's left shoulder and side were a mess, his shirt blood-soaked. What was more, the husky driver looked about ready to pass out. Sam ran and caught him just before he fell and lowered him to the ground. Kneeling beside him now and supporting him Sam said,

'What happened, Sol?'

Pierson's usual deeply tanned round face was pale and strained with pain. He looked up. 'Gang of five hit us in Gonzalez Pass, Sam. Meredith' — Meredith Seaton, Sam knew, was the shotgun guard on this run — 'wasn't having any of that and opened up with that Greener of his. He got off one shot and blew apart the arm of one of the road agents, but they drilled him afore he could unload his second charge and he fell down dead on to the trail.' Pierson paused, gasped, and grimaced as clearly a spasm of pain surged through him. Then he said, 'Well, I am not that brave, or that dumb, Sam, not with a wife and three kids to support, so I threw down the box. But they drilled me anyway, out of spite is my guess, for what Meredith did.'

Pierson paused, groaned with pain once more before he carried on, 'After that, I saw the writing on the wall and managed to get the horses running. Even so, they went on slinging lead until I was way out of range.'

Pierson's pain-filled, earnest stare now latched on to Sam's blue gaze as he clutched his arm. 'Sam, we lost the mailbag. We hit a fair-sized rock and it bounced high and wide, out on to the trail. Those no good snakes must have picked it up. Now, don't that make this a federal offence?'

Sam nodded grimly. He found a certain satisfaction in the news. 'It does and it gives me something to work on,' he said.

'Who were they, Solomon?' Vince Guthrie said, now coming down beside the driver. 'Did you see?'

'All masked up; couldn't tell,' Pierson said. 'Hell of it was, that was the Denison and Collins payroll I threw down, all fifteen thousand dollars of it.' Pierson's pain-racked eyes appealed to all three of them now. 'But what could I do, boys? They were sure out for blood after Meredith cut up rough.'

'You did all right, Solomon,' Vince said, 'you had passengers to consider. Dammit, no amount of money is worth a man's, or a woman's, life.'

Solomon Pierson looked clearly grateful for those reassuring words. 'I did my best,' he said, 'damned if I didn't.' It was then he passed out.

Sam called on two bystanders to carry Solomon to Doctor Bill Johnson's on Third Street. They obliged willingly. Solomon was a well known and liked character in Scar County and beyond.

It was then Frank Gorman came out of the stage office. Dave Bailey, the other partner of this well established firm, had died seven years before, Sam understood. However, Frank kept on the Gorman and Bailey name.

Frank Gorman was staring hard at Vince. 'Don't you think you'd better get a posse organized, Mayor? Dammit, the company can't keep taking these hits.

The insurers won't have it. These people must be caught and hanged for their crimes. It's getting to be a regular occurrence.'

Vince glared. 'D'you think you need to tell me that?' He stared around. 'Where the hell's the sheriff?'

At that moment county sheriff Mallory Grison came hurrying down the street. He was sided by one of his deputies, Roland P Smiley. Also with him was Graham Eccles, the editor and owner of the *Scar County Clarion*. All three men Sam had got to know during the short time he had been here.

When they arrived. Grison stared at Vince. 'What happened?'

Vince explained and editor Eccles took notes. When Vince was finished Grison said, 'And the mailbag fell off? You think they took that, too?'

Vince shrugged. 'It seems more than likely to me.'

Grison said, 'But, dammit, that makes it government business now.'

Sam, keeping his peace up until now,

said, 'Is that worrying you, Mal?'

Clearly made angry by that remark, Grison glared. 'Why should it? Being a federal man, that puts it in your bailiwick, not mine.'

Sam gave him his scar-distorted smile. 'A payroll was stolen, too, Mal. I figure that makes us partners in this. You going to form a posse?'

Grison looked at the crowd of people now gathered around the coach and the sweating and restless horses still harnessed to it. They were being gentled by one of Gorman and Bailey's stable hands prior to being lead away. Grison was obviously indignant.

'Dammit, of course I am. What d'you take me for?'

Malachi grinned, speaking for the first time, 'Well, if you don't mind, think I'll ride along, too, boys. Wouldn't want to miss the fun. Not only that, I reckon it will allow me to get acquainted with the country.'

Grison turned, saw the star on Malachi's chest and said, sourly, 'Well,

Malachi Curry, the new town marshall!'

Malachi broadened his grin, made a gun out of his thumb and forefinger, pointed it and said, 'Bang! Got it in one.'

Grison gave him a dirty look, opened his mouth to reply but Sam said, 'How about that posse, Mal, time's a wasting.'

Grison glared at him and waved an impatient hand. 'OK. OK. I'll get on to it.' He turned to his tall deputy. 'Get it organized, Roland. We gather outside the sheriff's office' — he pulled out his Waltham pocket watch and consulted it — 'make it in an hour's time. That will allow all likely volunteers to get armed, get victuals and get mounted.'

Replacing his pocket watch Grison looked at the large crowd of people now standing around. He said, with some gravity and not a little politicking, 'Rest assured, people, I aim to get to the bottom of this. I will not allow this sort of thing to happen in our county, or on our streets. It has already gone too far.' He turned to his deputy. He said,

'Dammit, Roland, are you still here? Get to sorting out that posse for Chris' sake.'

Tall, rangy Roland P Smiley stared for a moment, clear resentment on his face and then began walking up the street to do his boss's bidding.

Meanwhile, Sam said, 'Grison, I'll be heading out soon as I get my horse and vittles. I figure to be riding within fifteen minutes. I'll contact you if I find anything.' Malachi added, with a grin, 'I'm with you, brother. It's been mighty quiet down Mexico way lately and I do crave a little action.'

Grison did not seem to take kindly to the idea. He drew close. Looking at Sam, his voice barely above a whisper now he said, 'What do you hope to gain by this, Sam? Popularity? The all-action hero?'

'I hope to gain an hour on that posse you're organizing,' Sam said, equally as quietly. 'Gaining an hour could make the difference between catching those killers and losing them.'

Grison, obviously thinking that he was being upstaged in front of the voting public, hissed, 'You're mighty confident of that, aren't you?'

Sam said, 'Yeah, Mal, I am, but I will leave you a clear trail to follow if me and Malachi hit on anything.'

Clearly angry, Grison glared. 'I can do my own trailing, dammit!'

He turned on his heel and paced off up the street.

Sam watched him go, a small smile on his scarred lips. But it was no laughing matter; a man dead, one badly injured and killers running free.

He said, 'Come on, Malachi; we've got work to do.'

5

Twenty minutes later Sam and Malachi were on the Columbus-Hartville trail. In his saddle-bag Sam carried thick beef slices, coffee beans for two days and a large hunk of brown bread, all given to him by Mary Summerbee when he announced what he was about to embark upon. Before he left the boarding house Mary gripped his left stirrup, held on to it and looked earnestly up into his eyes. 'May God be with you in your endeavours, Mr Curry,' she said. She handed up the two large canteens of the well water he asked her to fill before he went to get his horse at Ed Brown's stables. Taken a little by surprise, but nevertheless touched by her sentiment, he said, 'Why, thank you kindly, ma'am.'

He passed one canteen to Malachi and hung his own on the saddle horn.

He touched the brim of his sombrero and prepared to say goodbye, but Mary Summerbee held on to his stirrup, her stare still intense. 'There be strong reasons for my words, sir. My husband died trying to farm this land — and he did, successfully, until . . .'

She paused. Her lips tightened into a thin line and her head went down. She whispered, 'Masked men came. They found my husband working in the fields. They lassoed him, dragged him behind their horses — it seemed forever. They were jeering and whooping, like it be carnival time.' She shook her head, her eyes pitifully sad as they looked up at him. 'It was horrible, sir, so horrible. My poor, dear Henry, who never done harm to any man. I still wake up at night hearing their shouting and my Henry's terrible screams.'

Again she stopped, as if to gather her demeanour, then went on, her voice almost a whisper, 'He survived the ordeal, sir, but he died three days later, all broken inside the doctor said.'

The story caused Sam's features to become stone like, look as though they had been hewn out of raw granite. His blue stare had also hardened to resemble chips of the hardest sapphire. He said, 'That is no way for a man to die, Mrs Summerbee. Were the raiders ever caught?'

Mary Summerbee shook her head. 'Sheriff Grison investigated but said they could find nothing to go on. He said this be big country; men experienced in such criminal ways could easily disappear into its vastness and be lost. But he did add he and his men would remain vigilant.'

Sam said, 'Well, a man can do only what he is capable of.'

Mary said, as if Sam's irony had escaped her, 'Yes, and I be still praying for him to catch those evil men.'

'I hope the good Lord grants your wish, ma'am,' Sam said. Again he touched the brim of his border sombrero. Malachi also touched his hat with similar courtesy and bobbed his head and said,

'Ma'am. It's been a real pleasure.'

Mary Summerbee stepped back, away from the horses. Sam and Malachi now urged their mounts down Fourth Street and on to the Hartville trail. But as Sam rode, Mary Summerbee's tragic story remained alive in his thoughts. There was no doubt about it — apart from finding Arthur's killer, there were other things that needed to be attended to here in Scar County. All hell was going on out there.

★ ★ ★

Gonzalez Pass proved to be rocky, treeless and desolate, a cauldron of stifling heat a man could hardly breathe in. When they arrived they found coyotes were tearing at Meredith Seaton's body.

Malachi downed one of the scavengers with his Winchester before they loped away, ears back, teeth bared, whining and yapping, into the rocks nearby to await the outcome of this

87

intrusion on their territory. The buzzards that were also gathered, ripping off chunks of flesh where they could while avoiding the snapping jaws of the coyotes, hopped away to play the waiting game too.

Sam saw Seaton's stomach cavity had already been torn open, his eyes pecked out and his entrails dragged out across the stony ground to be more easily ripped apart and gorged. Flies by the thousand were also feasting on his blood and flesh. No doubt about it, nature's burial party was here in full force. It was then Sam became aware that Malachi was looking at him with inquiring blue eyes.

'What d'you think? Bury him or leave him?'

Sam held his brother's quizzical gaze. 'Leave him.' He waved a hand at the waiting coyotes and buzzards. 'They've nearly got the job done already. I figure Grison's party will deal with what is left when they arrive. Longer we wait here, the harder it is going to be to pick up sign on those sons of bitches.'

Malachi grinned. 'Can't add to that.'

They found hoofs tracks all about in the sandy soil. And they found blood, a lot of blood. The driver, Pierson, said one of the hold up men had had his arm near blown off by lead from Meredith Seaton's shotgun. If that was the case, Sam decided, it was more than an even bet that man was now dead or very close to it. And his dying could quite possibly be slowing up those sons of bitches, if they had any compassion at all.

They started circling and expanding, like ripples in a placid stone-hit pool. Sam soon found promising tracks. It looked to him as though the stage robbers were heading for the Lonesome range, looming large and black to the northeast. He guessed there were maybe six of them. But the Lonesomes . . . that was not good news. That immense pile of rock was the most challenging of the three ranges, there was no doubt about that. But, hell, he'd been in worse situations, much worse over his law enforcement years.

He called to Malachi, 'Over here.'

Malachi joined him, his face unusually serious. Without words they followed sign out of the pass. They began to climb upwards, past huge boulders, stands of cottonwood and sycamore, up into the aspen and black pines and across fields of treacherous scree. It was hard work performed under a merciless sun that stared balefully out of a pitiless sky. Frequently they lost track and had to split and search over a wide area before they cut trail again.

It was an hour on they found the body of what had to be the wounded owlhoot. The arm Pierson must have hit was a mess, but Sam found his death was not due to that: the man had been shot through the head. It was clear he had become a burden and had been executed. Such ruthlessness he had encountered before, but even so his lips compressed and his blue stare hardened.

The country ahead became rougher — brush-choked ravines, some full of prickle bush — they had no other choice but to move around and more rock-strewn, treacherous slopes, the trail difficult to follow across them. It was with some relief, during late afternoon that they came upon a narrow grassy valley with a sweet-tasting stream running through it. Gratefully, they filled their canteens, drank their fill and allowed the horses to drink. It was a welcome oasis.

Come sunset, the sky streaked with gold and red and the air growing real cool at these heights, they were back amongst the rocks with stunted, wind-drawn spruce growing between them. Again, they lost sign. Malachi said, moodily, 'Dammit, this is a hell of a place. What do we do now?'

Sam shrugged. 'Eat, sleep and wait for sunrise?'

'You think that's a good idea?' Malachi said. 'We've plumb run out of sign with no clear chance of picking it up again.'

Sam said, 'You got a better notion?'

Malachi glared. 'Yeah, turn back and head for Columbus. Brother, in case you ain't noticed, we've hit a brick wall.'

Sam shook his head. 'Quitting is not yet on the agenda, Malachi. Right now we find a campsite, light a fire and eat Mrs Summerbee's beef and bread and drink her coffee. First light we start again.'

Malachi scowled at him. 'Always the stubborn cuss; Pa said it, Ma said it, Arthur said it, and now I'm saying it, dammit.'

Sam waited patiently for Malachi to finish his grump then said, 'Look at it this way, brother, from what I've heard, Sheriff Grison is giving up looking too easily. Well, we've got to prove to those robbing and murdering bastards out there we aren't like that, that we mean business, that real law has come to this county and we're it. We have got to send that message to whoever is causing the mayhem on this range and make it clear the heydays are over.'

Malachi squinted across the gloom of the descending night. He said, 'D'you reckon it is the cowboys that are causing the trouble?'

Having briefed Malachi on what he knew of the situation in Scar County during their long, hot search throughout the afternoon, Sam said, 'Vince Guthrie thinks so, and he's no fool, as you well know from the old days. Judging on what he has told me, that bunch down on Black Water Creek already want penning up in Yuma and the key throwing away, due to their shenanigans. Vince even reckons one of them killed Arthur. But that seems to be too pat for me, what I know so far. Oh! They're varmints, for sure, there's no denying that. But I think there could be somebody else pulling the real strings around here — especially with the stage hold-ups. There is a man with brains behind these operations and we've got to find out who it is.'

'You saying the cowboys have no brains?'

'I'm saying it ain't their style,' Sam said. 'Now, let's find a campsite, eat and get some sleep. We need to be fresh for morning.'

Malachi shook his head gloomily. 'Man, I'm beginning to wonder what the hell I've let myself in for. I could be bedding some fair *señorita* right now if I'd any sense at all.'

Sam grinned. 'You'll survive; you always have.'

Malachi growled his doubt about that.

6

At first light they ate the last of the bread and beef and drank the last of the coffee. After more tedious searching that lasted an hour or more, they finally found sign. However, to their further frustration, it petered out on the stony high ground where no trees grew and thin snow still lay in the bottoms of the gullies. No amount of searching caused them to discover further tracks.

After a couple of hours Malachi said, as if releasing his irritation, 'God damn them! They must know this country backwards and sideways!' Despite the coolness of the air at this altitude, he took off his border sombrero and wiped his perspiring brow on his coat sleeve.

Sam found he could not add to that, other than to say, 'Best get back to Columbus,' he said. 'Maybe Grison has come up with something.'

'And maybe not,' Malachi said, 'from what I'm hearing.'

Thoroughly dissatisfied they moved down the long, steep hillside, picking their way around boulders and low growing, barely surviving scrub oak and spruce toward the lower, more deciduous woodland. As they travelled, they welcomed the warmer air wafting up through the trees from the flat country below. They continued their slow descent until an hour later they entered a long, fertile valley.

A wide stream ran all the way through it, obviously topped up by the last of the melt water still draining out of the drift snow on the tops of the mountains. At the brook side they dismounted, drank their fill, watered the horses and filled up their canteens.

It was while they were doing this that Sam noticed two riders break out of the trees a quarter of a mile away, beyond the meadowland. They came cantering towards them. Out of long habit, Sam loosened the retaining loop over the hammer of his Colt and watched their approach with careful eyes. He decided, when they got up close, that their stares were not friendly. Malachi was also discreet in making his Smith & Wesson available for instant use. But there was a grin on his face . . . developed by the imminent possibility of gunplay.

When the riders were close enough he said, 'Well, howdy, boys? What can we do for you?'

The tall one with the thick black walrus moustache, the well worn range clothes and soulful spaniel-brown eyes said, without preamble, 'This here is Double Six land, mister, and you're trespassing.'

Sam shrugged easily and toyed with the reins. 'Just passing through, boys, no harm done.'

But the name Double Six rang a bell. Tom Lacy, one of the guests lodging for the night at Mary Summerbee's when he first arrived in Columbus, he said he ran the Double Six, out on the Rio Poco. This broad, deep stream they had just drunk from must be the Rio Poco. As Lacy said, a small river it wasn't.

The speaker for the two riders now drew his Colt, surprising Sam as well as Malachi. Sam narrowed his gaze at the sight of the exposed gunmetal. He said, 'No need for that, fellow. Like I said, we're just passing through.'

The man raised his thick, dark brows. 'Even so, you'll need to explain that to the boss. He don't like strangers riding in.'

'That'll be Tom Lacy,' Sam said.

The cowboy's look of hostility turned to one of guarded interest. 'You know him?'

Sam nodded. 'We've met.'

The rider turned to his companion. 'What d'you think, Slim?'

Slim, Sam saw, was a fat, bulbous-eyed fellow with a pugnacious cleft chin and smallpox cavities over most of his face. He also sported a huge black moustache like his partner. However, he only carried a Winchester and it was out of harm's way, in its saddle boot.

Sam could see no sidearm.

'Better take them in,' Slim said, 'that's our orders.' Then his eyes widened and he yelled, 'Jesus! Jed! Look out!'

The man holding the gun turned, with a gasp. He looked into the bore of Sam's Colt, trained on a point between his brown eyes. Panic immediately filled Jed's round stare. He hoisted his arms, Colt still in his hand. 'God a' mighty, take it easy, friend; just obeying orders. We were meaning no harm.'

'Never turn your back on a man, Jed,' Sam said. 'Now, pass that weapon over to my pard here, then take us to meet your boss.'

Seemingly relieved he was getting off so lightly Jed passed the Colt to Malachi like it was hot steel straight out of the furnace. He said, 'Sure, sure, mister, right now. Just take it easy.'

Sam nodded. 'Easy it'll be, Jed, if you behave. Now lead on.'

'Sure, sure,' Jed said, urgently.

★   ★   ★

99

Sam found the Double Six ranch house was under the pines and aspens at the north end of this long, fertile valley. The groups of beeves they passed were grazing on grama and timothy grass. Sam decided it was a modest spread, but it was obviously well run. Everything about it was neat and tidy and the pasture was not overgrazed. As they rode up the incline toward the log ranch house, Tom Lacy came out on to the stoop. He awaited their arrival. Sam saw four children were playing outside the house, two boys and two girls, ranging from about three upwards to twelve was Sam's best guess. The two girls and a boy were amusing themselves on a swing rigged up at the side of the house, the rope tied to the limb of a cottonwood, a cushion placed over the bend in the rope for a seat. What looked to be the oldest boy was practising roping, using a corral post as a steer's head.

As they approached, the children stopped their play and stood staring.

Close to the tie rail in front of the stoop Jed said, 'Found them down by the river, boss. They kind of got the drop on us.'

'Kind of, hell,' Malachi said.

Sam holstered his Colt.

Lacy's eyelids narrowed and he frowned. Sam met his grey stare as it turned on to him. Lacy said, 'Sam Curry? What are you doing in this neck of the woods?'

Sam told him about the hold up in Gonzalez Pass, the death of Meredith Seaton and the wounding of Solomon Pierson. He saw no reason to do otherwise; this was official business he was about. He finished, looking keenly at Lacy. 'D'you know anything about that killing and hold up, Lacy?'

The Double Six owner stared, clearly offended. He protested, 'Why the hell should I? I run a ranch, not a den of thieves.'

'Got to be somebody,' Sam said. He turned to the two hands. 'You know anything about it?'

Both shook a negative. Slim said, 'A hell of a thing, though. I know Sol Pierson real well.'

Malachi, quiet up until now, said, 'A hell of a thing, boys, sure enough.' He turned to the Double Six owner. 'Don't you think so, Lacy?' Malachi's grin flashed white through his dark moustache and the three days' growth of beard. 'Oh! My name's Malachi Curry, by the way.'

Lacy said, with a firm nod, 'I know who you are, one of Bat Masterson's deputies. I saw you in action in Dodge City back in the late seventies, along with your brother Arthur. That was before you both joined your brother there in Hayes.' He waved a hand towards Sam. Lacy lifted his craggy chin. 'What I recall of those days, you did not treat those Texas cowboys any too well, Malachi Curry.'

Malachi's smile closed to a tight-lipped line and his eyelids narrowed over steel blue eyes. He said, tersely, 'They got what they deserved, friend.

Nothing more, nothing less.'

'That's a matter of opinion,' Lacy said. He turned his gaze on to Sam. 'I take it you're heading back to Columbus?'

Sam nodded. 'That's the plan.'

Then surprisingly, though with some hesitation, Lacy said, 'Well, you'd better climb down and eat. You've a long way to go yet.' He turned to the two hands. 'Slim, run their horses into the corral for now and give them a fork of hay and top up the water trough.'

Slim spat, clearly not liking the order but did not say so. Slowly, he climbed down off his roan and wrapped the rein over the tie rail.

Sam also dismounted, saying as he did, 'White of you, Lacy. Seems range etiquette ain't yet dead, here on the Rio Poco.'

The Double Six owner shrugged. 'Getting close to it, nonetheless, what with one thing and another.' However, he did not elaborate further.

Sam handed the reins of his horse to

Slim and Malachi did likewise. Slim led the mounts away and Jed made his way toward the barn, still riding his sturdy buckskin.

Inside the ranch house the Double Six owner introduced them to his wife, Jane. Sam saw a small, blonde, blue-eyed woman, in her late thirties, he guessed. He decided she was still pretty despite the rigours of life on a remote frontier ranch and giving birth to four children, no doubt in the most primitive of circumstances.

She smiled shyly.

Sam took off his border sombrero and said, 'Ma'am. I hope we're not putting you to any trouble.'

'No trouble,' Jane Lacy said, 'we don't get many visitors.'

But it was a strained meal of ham and eggs they ate, though Lacy did become a little more amenable after a while and Jane Lacy, amiable from the start, wanted to know all the latest news circulating the county. And the children gathered to hang around the open door peeping curiously in, one of the girls smiling shyly at Sam and Malachi on the occasions when their eyes met. Even so, within the hour, with directions as to the shortest route to Columbus, they were on the trail again.

As they rode the length of the valley they saw beeves wearing Mexican brands not yet blotted out. Putting two and two together Sam came up with the opinion they were rustled cattle, sold cheaply to the ranchers hereabouts — possibly by none other than the thieving Wright Gang. Sam knew it was a common enough practice on both sides of this lawless border country. Apparently, most ranchers did not seem to see a great deal wrong with this illicit trade. Their feelings were that greaser cattle were greaser cattle and thus fair game. Indeed, Sam was sure, if they were asked about their participation in this criminal traffic, they would bitterly complain those bean eaters took enough Arizona cattle across the river, so why shouldn't they take their share of Mexican beef when the opportunity arose?

As he rode, Sam found himself shaking his head. The fact was, he was one of those ranchers below the line, although he was too far south to be troubled overmuch by Anglo rustlers. Mexican *bandidos*, yes, they were endemic. But, whatever, it was a crazy situation and it caused a good deal of hate to fester along that troubled border.

7

It was night when the two of them rode up Columbus's Main Street and dismounted outside the marshal's office.

The place was in darkness and Sam was mildly surprised by that. He was half expecting Vince Guthrie to be holding the fort while they were out, being an ex-lawman, or, at the very least, to have appointed somebody to do it. But there was probably a perfectly good reason why Vince had overlooked the arrangement and would tell it, if asked, which Sam fully intended not to do because, with a man of Vince's experience, he knew he could trust him to make the right decision. Even so, he remained slightly taken aback by the omission. This was a rip-roaring frontier town. It still needed law officers to hold the fort while the sheriff's posse was out and the town marshal was absent. But, hell, why should Sam Curry take on that worry? He had enough of his own.

Sam looked around at the near-deserted street. All seemed quiet. Perhaps he was making a mountain out of a molehill, being overzealous, as he knew all too well he could be on occasion. And what the hell was he doing here at the marshal's office at this time of night anyway? Soon as he rode into town any sensible man would have stabled his horse and made his way to his lodgings.

Any sensible man.

He dismounted wearily, Malachi likewise. They were entering the law office when the familiar sound of flying lead hissed past hair-thin close and then, immediately after, they heard the crack of rifles and the sound of glass shattering and of bullets splintering into the thin timbers of the office ahead of them.

Long-nurtured self preservation sent

Sam and Malachi to the dusty board-walk. Now flattened against it they crawled up behind separate awning supports. Malachi was already firing, the sharp crack of his Smith & Wesson American snapping echoes across the dark night.

Sam lined up his Colt aiming at the gun flashes coming from the dark maw that was Third Street across the wide Main Street they had ridden up only moments ago. The din of gunfire lifted to a roaring racket. Sheer chaos reigned for some seconds before a sharp cry of pain came from across the street. Almost immediately the firing ceased and there was a flurry of urgent, muted talk.

Taking advantage of the pause, Sam commenced reloading his seven-inch barrelled Colt, the ejected brass tinkling on to the boards near to eye level before him. Malachi was doing likewise.

Loaded again, Sam said, 'What d'you make of it?'

Malachi shrugged his big shoulders

and peered through the poor streetlight. 'Sounds to me like we hit one.'

Then, surprising both of them, came the sound of men's boots clattering down Third Street's boardwalk. Malachi, triumph in his eyes as he stared across the intervening space, said, 'By God, I believe they're running.'

Sam was already on his feet. He commenced to do an Indian run across the wide, dust-deep Main Street toward Third Street. Malachi followed. A side glance told Sam there was the usual taut grin across his brother's lean face now they were in action again. Sam shook his head. Even though Malachi was forty years of age it was clear he still possessed the appetite for this kind of thing, that the excitement was ambrosia to him. Just one crazy son of a gun, always had been!

Halfway across Main Street, they split, each scurrying into the cover of the trading establishments lining Third Street. Now hidden in the shadows of butcher Jim Post's shop doorway Sam stared through the star-and-lamp lit gloom to the other side of the street. Malachi, he saw, was in the darkness of Harry Meadows Gun and Ammunition Store, Repairs Done While You Wait.

As usual, Malachi's weapon was up by the side of his face ready at an instant's notice to level and aim. Sam switched his gaze to take in the whole of Third Street. As far as he could tell, it was deserted. Now he looked down at the boardwalk for possible clues. He was soon rewarded. The shape of boot marks in the quarter inch of dust covering the walkway, and a trail of blood that went with them, told Sam they had hit one of the bushwhackers and that they were not imagining it.

Tingling with excitement he whispered across the street, 'Something.'

In a voice Sam could barely hear Malachi said, 'Blood?'

'Uh, huh.'

Taking a fresh grip on his weapon Sam moved cautiously forward. Not fifteen steps later he found another dark trail joining the first signs of blood, making it two trails. *Two trails?* There were two hits?

He continued to follow their course. Seventy five yards on, one of the trails headed toward the rear door of Campbell's Long Bar, the other carried on down Third Street toward the Mexican adobes clustered at the southern end of town and forming a maze of back streets that eventually led to the Mexican quarter's main plaza.

Sam knew it was decision time. He looked across the street and called Malachi over. When his brother arrived beside him Sam pointed at the separating blood trails and said, 'What d'you think?'

After some scrutiny, Malachi lifted out a coin and tossed it. Catching it he stared at the result through the star-and-lamp shine. 'Heads says Mexico.'

Sam felt dissatisfaction. 'Dammit, Malachi, you know chance don't sit right with me in matters of this sort. I want your considered opinion.'

Malachi said, 'Well, you've got it. Dammit, whatever decision we come up with it's going to be a gamble, ain't it?'

Sam glowered through the dark. 'Instinct is telling me it's the Long Bar.'

Malachi shrugged. 'OK, it's the Long Bar. What's the difference?'

'A lifetime of experience,' Sam said, 'that's the difference.'

'Bullshit, brother! It's a gamble, no more, no less.'

Sam snorted, 'Watch my back, dammit. *I'm going in.*'

The blood trail heading for the Long Bar dripped its way through the rear entrance. With care, Sam tested the street door and found it was unlocked. Still with caution, he opened it and peered into the gloom. He saw it was a storeroom and that it was deserted. With the door now open, the former muted tinkle of the saloon piano they could hear when it was closed now became louder. It was banging out a hymn and there was the raucous chorus of drunken men singing to the rousing tune. Sam assumed they must be the Welshmen, or the Cornishmen, or both, who made up a large minority of the men working at the diggings. Possibly, they were singing to remind themselves of their homeland and the loved ones they left behind when they came to this New World to make their fortunes before they sent for them. Sam also knew there were English miners here as well. English, Welsh, Cornish, Scottish . . . most brought over by British speculators who were exploiting to the full the wealth to be found here in the New World.

With Malachi, Sam entered the dismal storeroom. They crossed the creaking floor to the closed door at the other end. Sam saw light was shining yellow through the gaps around the door edges. Sam confidently assumed this door would give him entrance to the main saloon beyond. While Sam closed up on the door, Malachi edged to the side of it, his Smith & Wesson double-action, as usual, held high, by his right car. Malachi whispered, 'Same routine, brother?'

Sam nodded. He opened the door slightly. After the gloom of the storeroom and the night beyond it, the sudden shard of bright light issuing from the saloon momentarily dazzled him. When he was accustomed to the glare he was happy to observe no one was looking his way: the sweaty crowd were either singing or listening to the singers, while swinging their glasses of rotgut or beer to the rhythm of the robust hymn. He slid unobtrusively in; his concentration fully centred on the job at hand, the trail of blood that was leading across the large, stiflingly hot room.

He paused. The crowd was still distracted by the singing. His gaze took in the stage at the top end of the long saloon. That was where the chorus girls strutted their stuff twice nightly; where the singing, dancing and the comedy acts, mostly shipped in from the East, went through their nightly routines. At present the curtains were drawn.

Detaching his gaze now Sam saw Hiram Campbell, the bluff owner of the premises, was leaning his broad back against the long bar. Smug satisfaction was stamped on his brick-red face as he surveyed the scene around him: the poker-playing cowhands; the garishly made up percentage girls, the drunken singing miners. Towards the middle and other side of the big room were the faro, roulette and other gaming tables. Despite the holy singing, the gaming tables were still doing brisk business. And all this under the brilliant light coming from the two crystal chandeliers Hiram Campbell had shipped in from New Orleans not six months ago.

Hiram was smiling benignly upon his customers, two fingers stuffed into each of the two pockets of his colourfully embroidered vest. Indeed, Hiram appeared to be well pleased with what he was looking at. And, as always, he looked real smart in his brown, pinstriped suit and brown string tie, suspended from the collar of his frilly-fronted white shirt. His brightly polished brown elastic-sided boots finished off his prosperous appearance. It was obvious Hiram was extremely pleased that business was so brisk on this usually quiet Wednesday night.

As Sam approached the saloon owner, Hiram became aware of him and smiled. He said, amiably, 'Well, thought you were out hunting murderers, Deputy. Buy you a drink?'

Sam nodded and said, 'Thanks. I'll have a beer.'

Campbell waved an arm to one of the busy 'keeps and ordered the brew. The beer duly arrived and Hiram slid the brimming schooner over to Sam, offering a further toothy smile. 'I've got to say; we don't see much of you in here, marshal, except in an official capacity. So, what brings you here now, and through the back way.'

Vigilant Mr Campbell!

Sam took a long grateful drink of the beer and then pointed to the blood trail across the floor. 'I'm following that,' he said. 'I've reason to believe it belongs to one of the men who tried to bushwhack me and my brother out on the street just now.' Campbell raised dark brows as if he was surprised. 'So that was what the shooting was all about.'

Sam nodded. 'Got it in one.'

Campbell said gravely, 'Well, I'm sorry to disappoint you, Deputy, but you've got to be wrong there. My dog made those stains not five minutes ago; saw it myself. The mutt must have been fighting again.' Campbell shook his head. A wry smile formed on his fleshy lips. 'He's a real mean critter is that one. He'd fight his own shadow if he'd got nothing else to tooth and claw at.'

'Even so, it's curious,' Sam said, 'for tracks — boot and blood — led straight into here. Does your dog wear boots?'

Campbell lost his smile. 'You being funny, Deputy?'

'No,' Sam said, his blue stare icy. 'It ain't in my nature when I'm hunting down killers.'

Campbell frowned as if puzzled. 'Boot marks?' He rubbed his chin and knitted the ends of his thick brows, as if thinking hard on that. Then he said, 'Well, of course there's boot marks. Bound to be. Stock is coming in daily; men are walking in and out of that back room all the time. Sure there'll be boot marks. It stands to reason, don't it? But nobody's come through that door tonight, Deputy, apart from you and that mutt of mine. He scratched and I let him in myself.'

'Even so, you won't mind if I keep following that trail,' Sam said, 'just in case it ain't the mutt and it leads me to one of the bastards that has been shooting at us?'

Campbell shrugged his indifference. 'Suit yourself, but you won't find anything, only what I say.'

Sam now became aware the room was going quiet and that the singing was tailing off. It was as though people were realizing that there might be things of a more exciting nature than singing hymns in the offing. And in most cases that would be welcome. A bout of no-holds-barred fisticuffs for these rough, tough men would undoubtedly round off a good night of drinking and singing real well.

Sam tried to ignore the building tension and followed the blood trail. It took him past a particular table with five cowhands sitting around it, shot glasses at various stages of emptiness, fans of cards in hand. Cigarette smoke hung thickly overhead; the game they were playing was obviously poker. And Sam knew these boys.

John Wright, the big man with the large tawny eyes, amiable features and the brown walrus moustache sprouting from under his big nose, was sitting closest to him and was staring up at him. Wright was saying, 'Well now, look it here, boys, if it ain't that old law dog Deputy US Marshal Sam Curry.'

Sam stared into the cattle rustler's apparently cordial brown gaze, but he did not miss the heavy sarcasm that was in Wright's voice. Before he spoke he surveyed the other four players around the table: Wild Man Haines, James Wright, Frank Norton and his brother Henry. The third brother, Jeff, was stood off, watching the game.

'Kind of curious to know what you are doing here, boys?' Sam said.

The owner of the Blue Jay held up his hands, his face a picture of innocence. 'Why, playing some cards, Marshal. It's what me and the boys do occasionally. Have you got any objections to that?'

'No objections, if you keep your noses clean,' Sam said. 'But while you're here you can answer some questions. Were you and your boys anywhere near Gonzalez Pass yesterday?'

John Wright hooted genuine laughter. He looked into the four other faces around the table. 'Did you hear that, boys? Deputy US Marshal Sam Curry here wants to know if we were anywhere near Gonzalez Pass yesterday!'

'Too damned hot for me in that hole,' Wild Man Haines said. He leered around at the others at the table. 'How about you, boys?'

Haines was a big man with strong, resolute features and hard amber-coloured eyes. His usually fiery red hair was muted to a tamer ginger colour under the bright light of the chandelier above his head.

James Wright, peering with bold eyes over his fan of cards, said petulantly, 'The hell you asking us for, Curry?'

'Seems the logical thing to do,' Sam said, 'seeing as you've got a reputation. Another thing, any of you know about these bloodstains?'

He pointed to the marks on the floor.

Frank Norton, tall, lean as a beanpole, eyes as pale as river ice in winter said, with an oafish grin thinning his already lean lips, 'Maybe one of the girls is on a bad day an' forget to put her towels on?'

Raucous guffaws came from the five owlhoots. Henry Norton said, 'Now ain't you just the joker, Frank?' He grinned broadly at Sam. 'What do you reckon, Deputy? Ain't Frank the joker?'

'He's a foul mouthed son of a bitch is my opinion.'

Frank Norton's pale eyes set hard as diamonds and he stood up, hand hovering over his the butt of his belt weapon. Sam remembered Vince Guthrie warning him a week ago that Frank fancied himself as a gunfighter. And, sure enough, Frank was saying, 'By God, I don't have to take that from any man, federal lawman or no. Take off that damned badge you're hiding behind, Curry, and come out on to the street. We'll see who is the big man around here.'

John Wright said, waving a languid hand, 'Aw, sit down, Frank, ain't nothin' to break into a sweat over.'

Frank glowered and growled but reluctantly sat down. Sam decided that established who was the alpha male in this wolf pack.

Sam now felt the full force of John

Wright's brown eyes upon him. He found nothing amiable about those big orbs now. Wright said, 'Have you finished here, Deputy? Like I told you, we don't know anything about that blood trail and we don't know anything about Gonzalez Pass, or the death of Meredith Seaton, or the wounding of Solomon Pierson. Have you got that?'

Sam smiled, knowing the terrible scar down his face would make it a ghoulish leer. 'You don't seriously expect me to believe that, do you, John?'

The eldest Wright looked real hot and angry now. 'Damned right I do, coming in here accusing law-abiding folk. Just ain't right, ain't right at all. You're getting to be just like your damned brother — allus accusing.'

Wild Man Haines said, 'Get this, friend, we're legitimate horse dealers. Now stop pestering us.'

Sam stared at him. 'You . . . did you kill my brother Arthur?'

Haines reared up out of his slump. He poked a finger into his chest and leaned forward. 'Me? My, God, you got a damned nerve. What would I want to do that for?'

'Arthur shot Arkansas Jack Reed, one of your men. Good enough reason, wouldn't you say?'

'Reed was acting on his own behalf, not ours,' Haines said then he glared, his look fierce. 'Dammit, have you come in here to make trouble, Deputy?'

Sam shrugged. 'Read it how you will.'

John Wright said, 'Shit, you really believing we did for your brother? If you is, you got to be living in dreamland.'

Sam said, 'I leave nothing out.'

The rest of his words were interrupted by the harsh crack of a sixgun. The noise came from the storeroom doorway. A harsh yell issued from the landing, above the saloon floor — a platform that permitted access to the row of whores' bedrooms lined up there. A broad stairway led up to them from the saloon floor.

The boom of a rifle accompanied

the yell and the shatter of glass. Then came the sound of timber breaking. Looking up, Sam saw the banister along the landing preventing people from falling was breaking under the weight of a fellow who was now toppling through it, blood red on his chest, down on to the gaming table directly below him. Glass from the bullet-shattered chandelier above the table the Wright boys were sitting around was now showering down, along with flaming oil. With harsh cries the Wright gang were staggering back, howling and batting at the liquid flames. It was chaos.

Slick as a well greased machine, Sam had his Colt out and covering the table he was standing by. However, the Wright boys were too intent on trying to kill the flames, by beating at them to pay attention to him. He swept the room with a bleak, icy-blue stare, trying to take in what had happened. He picked out Malachi. He was standing exposed, framed in the storeroom doorway. His Smith & Wesson double-action was fanning across his midriff, generally covering the startled people in the room. When Malachi saw Sam was looking at him he called above the din.

'That son of a bitch up there was drawing a bead on you.'

Sam turned and automatically stared at John Wright. He was now standing by the table, still batting at smouldering patches on his range gear. Sam said, 'You got anything to do with this?'

John Wright looked at him, genuinely puzzled. Other people around the table quickly recovered their demeanour. Wright said, 'Honest to God, Deputy, how in the hell were we supposed to know you would be coming in here tonight?'

Sam said, 'You tell me.'

Wild Man Haines said, 'Why, you son of a bitch — back off, we had nothing to do with this.'

Sam said, 'I'm not believing you.'

Haines glared. 'Well, be damned then, for you've got the truth.'

Sam stared around the taut, pale faces of the crowd now. Clearly, they, too, were in shock. Sam pointed at the dead rifleman sprawled on the floor by the shattered card table. '*Anybody know him?*'

A man near the body said, 'It's Big Mouth Bartlett. He's from up north of the county, cowhand and part time owlhoot and I guess it don't matter to talk about him now he's dead.'

Sam looked around at the sea of faces. 'Is that all?'

'What else is there?' called the man. 'Big Mouth was just a bum with a chip on his shoulder size of a log. Allus gave the impression he thought the world owed him a living and was real put out when he found out it didn't. I rode with him a couple of times, once at the Crossed R up near Clayton's Crossing, another time at the Double Six, on the Rio Poco, Tom Lacy's place.'

Sam said, 'Was he a bushwhacker?'

The man said, his nerves clearly settling now, 'Dammit, how should I know? But I guess he'd try his hand at most anything if the money were right. Big Mouth sure weren't particular when it came to money.'

Sam slid his gaze on to Hiram Campbell, still leaning on the bar, but looking pale.

'Campbell? What have you got to say?'

'About Big Mouth?'

'Who else, dammit?'

Campbell shrugged, pursed his purple lips and said, 'Most of the time he just rode in, got stinking drunk and rode out again.'

'Damn pity he missed you is all I got to say,' Frank Norton now said, recovered from being showered with flames and glass. 'Had it have been me I'd have nailed you good.'

Sam swung around, stepped forward, and with a vicious sideswipe laid his Colt barrel across Frank's sullen face. Blood spurted from the cowboy's mouth and cheek and he staggered back with a yell, clawing for his belt weapon. But the clicks of Sam arming his sidearm delayed the draw mid-reach and Frank crouched there, glowering, his face dripping blood and filled with pure hate.

Sam slid his Colt into its holster. He said, 'Are you feeling lucky, Frank? Then go ahead. Reckon I've evened it up now.' He held his hands wide and waited.

Frank Norton glared at him. Murder was clearly on his mind, meanness in every fibre of his body. With a trembling hand he tried to wipe away the blood rolling down his face. 'D'you take me for a fool?' he breathed. 'I can't see, dammit. Hitting me has blurred my vision. But, by God, there'll be another day. By a country mile, lawman, this ain't finished.'

'It'd better be,' Sam said. He looked at the rest of them around the table. 'Anybody else want to take this up?'

There were vicious stares, sullen stares all directed straight at him but nobody took up his challenge. Wild

Man Haines said, 'Seems nobody is in the mood to take you on right now, Deputy. All we came in for was a game of cards.'

'Ain't your style, huh?' Sam said. 'But ambushing a man is.'

Haines glared. 'By God, man, you're pushing it.'

Showing his contempt Sam turned and stared around the room. 'Anybody see a wounded man pass through here just now? Other men?'

There was a moody silence before Hiram Campbell broke it. 'You've got all the facts there is on that one, Deputy. Nobody's been through here, bleeding or otherwise. It was my mutt, and he's gone outside.'

Sam stared toward Malachi. He saw his brother was now hidden in the shadows of the storeroom again but light glinted off his levelled Smith & Wesson, which was still covering the room. He waved a hand at the Wright gang. 'Cover these sons of bitches until I'm out of here, Malachi.'

'Will do.'

Sam backed, all the way to the swing doors. He went through them, following the trail of blood, sure in the knowledge that Malachi would be protecting his back. No doubt about it he had made some enemies just now. But, what was new about that, for God's sake?

8

Outside, Sam followed the blood trail. He found Campbell's big, rangy mutt a short way along the boardwalk. It was lying against Cohen's Haberdashery and Tailoring, Fine Suits Made to Measure. The mutt was licking a bad wound in its side. It looked to Sam as though the animal had tangled with a critter meaner than he was and hadn't got the better of the exchange. But he was bitterly disappointed to find Campbell's tale about the dog was true. Judging from the cry they heard he was sure either he or Malachi had hit one of those bushwhacking sons of Satan and this was the trail they should follow.

He made his way to the wide alley that led to the back of Campbell's Long Bar. He found Malachi was waiting for him in the shadows, near the storeroom door.

Sam had half expected some sort of reaction from within the saloon by now, like the whole of the Wright gang, or Frank Norton in particular, following him into the street to call him out. But it had not happened and he relaxed the tension that had built up in him because of that expectancy. When he got up close Malachi said, 'Judging by the look on your face you backed the wrong horse.'

Sam admitted, 'Got to be the Mexican quarter.'

'They'll be long gone, brother,' Malachi said.

'Still got to follow it through.'

Malachi chuckled quietly and said, 'Would have been disappointed if you had said otherwise.'

They picked up the second blood trail. It wound through tarpaper shacks then across trash-filled ground to the adobes of the Mexican quarter. There they crossed the small plaza with the church and passed one of the two cantinas. From it came the strum of a guitar and the soulful voice of a woman. It was a song that spoke of love, of suffering, of long years of oppression, of brave resistance — a strange mixture of all four and oddly beautiful in its rendition.

The trail of blood went past the cantina and out toward the sage and scrub and cactus flatlands. It was now clear, judging from the track they were following, that two men were dragging the wounded man, one on each arm, and none too gently.

After a further three minutes, eyes straining to make as much as possible of the faint silver starlight they were working by now, they came upon the milling hoof prints of at least five horses. Obviously, they had been held there while the attempt at getting rid of the Curry brothers had been tried.

Sam looked at his brother. 'Dammit, we seem to be hitting nothing but brick walls.' He sighed. 'Well, there's nothing to be done here. We'd better get back to the office, collect the horses and bed them down for the night and then go get some sleep. We'll pick up this trail in the morning.'

Malachi said, 'At least we've cleared up one thing; it couldn't have been the Wright boys . . . they were in the Long Bar.'

Sam rubbed his chin pensively. 'Yeah. But who else on this range wants our hide so badly, Malachi?'

Malachi shrugged. 'That's the big question.'

When they got back to the office they found Vince Guthrie was there, lounging in the worn leather and scarred wood swivel chair. His amber stare was clear and direct and met Sam's blue gaze head on as Sam came through the door. He had a half-smile on his face. 'Hear they've been using you as a target, Sam.'

Finding nothing amusing in it Sam said, 'We found their trail but, as well you know, in this dark we can't do nothing with it 'til morning.' He took off his sombrero and scratched his itching scalp. 'How did Grison get on?'

Vince pursed his lips. 'Still out; seems he means business this time.'

Sam felt a hint of satisfaction to receive that information; Grison finally getting down to the task he was paid to do. He said, 'That's something, I guess.'

Vince nodded. 'Also heard you had a run in with the Wright boys.'

Sam said, 'Nothing we couldn't handle.' He frowned now. 'You're kind of late out, aren't you, Vince? You want something?'

Vince got up out of the chair and Malachi sank down into it and started inspecting his nails. After the perusal he took out his belt knife — a big Bowie — and started trimming them and scraping the dirt from under them. The ease of the paring suggested to Sam the knife was razor sharp. It did not surprise him.

Vince was saying in answer to his question, 'I've been up in the Consolations looking over my mining interests. Got back an hour ago. Was having

137

coffee in the Ace in the Hole when I heard the shots. Made some inquiries then came here to wait to find out how you'd got on. The thing is, boys, the town's governing committee meet at nine o'clock tomorrow. I was hoping you would have some good news I could give them. They badly want results.'

Sam stared. 'And they think we don't?' he said, his tiredness leaking into his voice. He was trying hard to hide his frustration after another day and night out with damn all to show for it. 'You know it isn't as easy as that, Vince. Dammit, you did the job long enough.'

Vince said, '*I* know that, but they don't.'

'Then tell them we're following up some leads.'

Vince stared. 'Are you?'

Sam shrugged. 'Wish I could say yes, but I can't. However, it might hold them for a spell.' He then told his friend about the blood trail through the

Mexican quarter and their intention to follow it up in the morning.

Vince still looked doubtful. 'Not much to go on,' he said.

'It's as good as we're going to get right now.' Sam sighed and stretched his aching frame. 'Vince, I'm tired, so is Malachi. Is that all?'

Vince nodded. 'I guess so. I just wanted to know if you had something I could give to the committee. Seems you haven't.'

He nodded and looked from Sam to Malachi and back again. Sam thought Vince's face looked drawn and gaunt under the dirty oil lamp hanging above their heads. He found that unusual. Vince was as tough as they come; little fazed him for long. But, thought Sam a little mischievously, maybe the worries of the mayor's office and all that money he was making from his business interests, was beginning to get to him. Sam laughed inwardly at his own humour as he filed out behind Vince and Malachi, turned and locked up the marshal's office. He gave Malachi the key.

Now, to stable the horse and get some sleep. And in the morning:

What?

9

Sunup next morning Malachi and Sam were again in the saddle and following the trail they found the night before out into the dry country beyond the Mexican quarter. The deep indents in the sand-and-pebble ground made by restless hoofs were still visible after what had been a calm, windless night.

Near noon they topped out on a huge red outcrop jutting like the prow of a ship from a steep, rocky hill-side that reared up above the flat lands before the formations climbed ever higher to finally form into mountains. It was there they found a cairn of rocks with a body under it.

They dismounted and took the cairn apart. Sam stared down at the cadaver. He judged, using the experience gained from viewing dead bodies over a long period of time that, going on the bruise-like colouration on the under side of the cadaver's body — he was lying face down — this was a man that had been dead for some time. Possibly six hours, maybe more.

He was a stranger to both of them. They searched the pockets of his clothing, indeed, everything, but found nothing that could identify him. Whoever had left him here, Sam decided, had been thorough.

He scanned the desolate country beyond with keen eyes, towards the direction in which they were heading. The trail was becoming barely readable on the solid rock they were now on and he could see little movement out there, certainly not a group of men riding together, as he naïvely half-hoped might be the case. Deep disappointment filled him. Again, they appeared to be going nowhere and fast — those sons of bitches out there knew their business.

He turned his attention to Malachi. His brother was using the waiting time to take a long drink from his canteen.

He was clearly unhappy about the situation as well and, knowing him, Sam thought, he would soon make his unhappiness known. And he did. His thirst apparently satisfied, Malachi hung the canteen on his saddle horn, lifted his stare and said, 'Sam, I reckon greasers are far more civilized about heat than we are. Come noon they *siesta*. So, dammit, how about it? I'm burning up here.' With some disgust Malachi swept off his border sombrero and exposed his sweat-matted hair. He mopped his broad brow. 'Hell,' he continued, 'if you ask me, we need some damn Apache buck with us to do this job. For sure, we aren't up to it. And, dammit, I ain't ever claimed to be a real good tracker, nor have you, what I recall.'

Sam found he had to silently agree with his brother. He looked out at the desolate mountains and flat-lands, but kept his feelings of frustration and despair hidden. He said, 'I agree, but we keep going, Malachi. One thing is for sure: above all else, I aim to catch Arthur's killer or die in the trying. And if grinding this out is going to take me to that killer, all well and good.'

Malachi's look was indignant. 'And you reckon *I* don't want that?'

'I *know* you do,' Sam said, 'so, come on.'

With a click of his tongue he urged his mount toward the long rocky upland at the back of the outcrop. Malachi followed, muttering about heat, damned flies and murdering sons of bitches needing to be strung up by their private parts and left to rot there until hell froze over!

Eventually, they picked up more positive sign. It headed for the Lonesomes, which were rearing their sharp peaks in the northern distance.

By mid-afternoon, on more rocky ground, the sign petered out again, but they kept going, right on into the heart of the mountains using instinct and little else. Toward evening Malachi said he thought he saw the glint of sun on steel about a mile ahead, but only for a second or two. That, Sam decided, was unusual in this vast hinterland — sun on steel. However, it could be prospectors; they did get to some of the loneliest places on earth in their insatiable quest for precious metals. But, on the other hand, it could be the men they were looking for . . .

Late evening, Malachi shot a rabbit. Come night, by a small creek, they made camp. Malachi skinned the rabbit, cooked it and they ate, Mary Summerbee's packed victuals having been eaten earlier in the day. Only some bread was left and half a bag of coffee beans. For all his grumping and distaste for the wilder country, Sam decided Malachi always was a good provider when they were on the trail. But then Malachi did have more than a little experience of the owlhoot trail, when things were not going too well in other directions. A strange mix was Malachi — a mix Sam did not always want to know about.

Food eaten they banked the fire and pulled up their blankets. Within minutes Malachi was snoring.

*　*　*

It was maybe an hour after midnight, Sam judged, when the quiet whinny from one of the horses brought him abruptly awake and fully alert. He remained still, tight, felt his throat going dry. He carefully gripped the butt of his Colt, placed handily under his saddle pillow before he went to sleep. He drew it. Still hyper-careful he leaned over and nudged Malachi gently in the back. His brother's head lifted slightly above his blanket but other than that he hardly moved. His voice barely a whisper he said, 'Yeah?'

'Think we got visitors.'

The horses were moving even more restlessly now. Sam slid out of his blanket and bulked it up to make it look as though a man was still sleeping in it. Malachi did the same. Each knew the drill and went off in opposite directions to hide. When he was in the brush, Sam got into a position to enable Malachi and he to set up a murderous crossfire, then he settled down to wait.

They did not have to wait long. Sam heard whispers in the trees, coming from where the horses were picketed. He tensed and stared into the starlit night and wished for a moon strong enough to give them some shooting light.

He took a fresh grip on the walnut handle of his Colt. He licked his dry lips and tried to ignore the sweat that was now forming on his broad forehead and was beginning to trickle down his back as well as moisten his palms. From across the clearing came the crack of a twig and the faint rustle of disturbed brush. Then Malachi was firing and almost immediately, there was a stifled yell.

Sam opened up now and then rolled a couple of yards to his left and once more faced up. Three guns answered his and Malachi's fire, but the attackers seemed confused — Sam one side of the gloomy clearing, Malachi the other. They did not seem to know which target to fire at first and, Sam knew, being caught in a crossfire like those sons of bitches were, was never going to make life comfortable.

Sam fired once more, moved, and fired again until his Colt was empty. Then he rolled and came up behind the trunk of a silver birch. He feverishly reloaded, ignoring the sweat that was trickling down his face.

Loaded again he peered into the gloom. Over the other side of the clearing Malachi was still firing. But then all went quiet in his direction, too, though the outlaw guns were still blazing away.

Sam guessed Malachi must also be reloading his weapon and because of that he was now vulnerable. Sam set to work with his Colt, using the flash of the bushwhackers' guns as an aiming point, and to take the pressure off

Malachi while his brother reloaded his weapon. But after that flurry, the firing from the intruders petered out.

Having no targets to aim at, Sam held his fire. He assumed they, too, must have been recharging their guns. However, he soon found — dammit, he already knew! — it was a mistake to use guesswork.

There was a rustling in the brush then some crazy bastard came bounding out of the undergrowth, his Colt spitting lead at Malachi's last known position. Clearly he was eager to take advantage of this present hiatus. Maybe he was thinking both Malachi and he were desperately attempting to reload, thus giving him an edge.

Cold satisfaction in him, Sam raised his Colt and fired. He was pleased to hear the man scream and see him bend and grasp his thigh. Then he was hobbling off into the night, shouting to the others to call it off and get the hell out of here.

Malachi now opened up, the report

from his Smith & Wesson double-action like the repeated cracks of a whiplash on the night: one, two, three! Over where the intruders were, there was a crashing through the bushes and harsh curses. Moments later, there was the heavy beat of hoofs in the night, which faded fast.

But Sam waited, his ears straining. Minutes later came the sharp repetitive call of a whippoorwill. That had to be Malachi, Sam decided. It was a routine from their early youth in the Missouri brakes. A minute later his brother came out of the night and joined him.

'All clear,' he said.

'Somebody wants us real bad, Malachi,' Sam said, sliding fresh bullets into emptied chambers.

'Inclined to agree,' Malachi said.

They went to where the horses were picketed: their mounts were gone. Malachi's lips thinned into a bitter line. 'If that doesn't beat all!' He threw his sombrero on to the ground. 'Sons of bitches!'

Sam said, 'I'm not so sure they took them. Maybe with all the noise the horses took fright, broke loose and bolted with the bushwhackers' horses when they left. If that's the case, mine will be back for sure. It's trained.' He looked at Malachi through the night gloom. 'How about you, Malachi?'

His brother cleared his throat. He even looked a little embarrassed. 'Mine's is ... er ... a recent acquisition and maybe it won't be coming back.'

Sam stared. 'You mean you stole it?'

Malachi could not look him in the eye. 'Well, not stole exactly. Borrowed would be a better word. Dammit, you wanted me here in a hurry, didn't you?'

Sam raised brows in exasperation. 'Jesus H Christ, Malachi! How old are you? And ain't you supposed to be on the right side of the law?'

Malachi said, 'Hell, Sam, there was more'n a hundred in that remuda I hit. I doubt if they'll miss one. And anyway, it was the other side of the border. So, who gives a shit about them?'

'Dammit,' Sam said, 'you stole it, Malachi!' He paused, sighed, heavily then added, 'Well, maybe it will stick with mine and follow it in. They seemed to get on together well enough. Meanwhile, we double up. Now, let's get some sleep. I don't figure they'll be back tonight.'

* * *

An hour before dawn, in the dark mountain cold, the two horses came back. They were steaming. Right off, Sam's horse nuzzled him and whinnied. Malachi's big strawberry roan began gnawing grass as if this was as good a place as any to graze and as if nothing unusual had happened; just a walk in the park.

Both relieved men caught them, fussed them, rubbed them down with grass and then walked them round until they were satisfied they were cool enough. After that, they tied them to rope long enough to allow some grazing. Then Malachi looked at the sky. 'Nearly dawn and I'm hungry, brother.'

'You think you've got a priority on that?' Sam said. 'But there ain't nothing to eat until we get back to Columbus.'

Malachi grinned. 'Yeah? Just give me an hour and liven up that fire, brother mine, and get some coffee going.'

Sam's look was hopeful. 'You going fishing?'

Malachi smiled and fumbled in his saddle-bag, pulling out his fishing line. 'What d'you think, brother? I'm a country boy just like you, only you haven't got a fishing line just now, have you? It must be a good life you're leading down on the San Luis, that's all I got to say.'

'Go to hell,' Sam said with a grin.

Chuckling quietly, Malachi went into the morning, which was becoming increasingly lighter in the east. Ten minutes under the hour Malachi was back holding catfish and trout. The sun was now fully up and the coffee was burbling. They cooked the fish and ate it as the sun rose above the mountains to bathe them in warm light. Malachi breathed deep of the pine-fragrant mountain air.

'Great to be alive, brother,' he said.

Despite it all, Sam could not help but agree.

10

Four hours later, the sun hot enough to fry eggs on a flat stone, Sam and Malachi were riding up Columbus's traffic-heavy Main Street, heading toward the marshal's office. At the tie rail they dismounted but neither of them was ready for the next disturbance in their lives.

As he dismounted Sam saw Frank Norton coming out of the Long Bar, whiskey bottle held in his left hand. Soon as Frank saw him he drew his Colt and fired twice into the stifling air. Then he whooped and returned his weapon to its holster. Re-holstering his own Colt, which he had drawn in a hurry expecting gun-talk, Sam stared across the street. Frank was swaying, looking as though he was carrying more liquor than was good for him. And there was a stupid grin on his face; a face that was black and blue, swollen with the bruises Sam put on it the other night. One thing was for sure; Frank Norton was well on the way to being legless drunk.

Sam said, 'What the hell were you doing, Frank, shooting off like that; I could have killed you.'

'But yah didn't.'

Traffic was now fast moving away from the scene, as were the horse riders and the numerous men and women walking the boardwalks. However, Sam hardly noticed the frantic activity; he was concentrated solely on Frank Norton.

He said, 'OK, so, what now, Frank?'

Grinning stupidly and swaying, Frank looked surprised. 'What now, for God's sake? Why, I'm going to kill you, dammit!'

Sam became aware that Malachi was coming into the periphery of his vision, left side. As usual in situations like this, Malachi had his killing smile on. He said, 'Leave him to me, Sam, I'll trim his damned sail.'

Sam shook his head, his gaze never

leaving Frank Norton. He said, his voice pitched low enough hopefully for Frank not to hear, 'This is my play, Malachi; you keep your eyes peeled for snipers, Frank's brother Henry in particular. I reckon those shots just now have got to be a signal.'

Malachi's look showed sudden enlightenment and he smiled. 'Yeah . . . as you say, brother.' He hefted the Winchester in his hand and lifted his gaze to meticulously search every nook and cranny atop of the false fronts opposite.

Meantime Sam called, 'Go home, Frank, you're drunk.'

The Blue Jay cowboy drank from his bottle and then leered across the street. 'Sober enough for you, by God!'

Now Sam began walking with measured steps across Main Street, his gaze holding Frank's whiskey-bugged stare. 'Give this up, Frank,' he said. 'We've got no quarrel you and I — not enough to die for, anyway.'

'The hell we haven't.' Norton pointed to the angry bruises on his face. 'How

about these, you no good son of a bitch!'
Then his grey stare widened and he
raised the hand with the bottle in it and
pointed a shaking finger. 'And just you
stay back, Goddamn you! I know your
tricks. You ain't going to pistol whip me
twice!'

Sam said, smoothly, 'So do the
sensible thing, Frank. Ride out and
we'll forget this.' But Frank was clearly
not about to do that. His face lost its
leer and became serious. He wiped his
right hand nervously across his bruised
lips and then he flicked a quick, anxious
glance across the rooftops. After that he
dropped the bottle in his left hand and
lowered both hands to his sides. Now
he began clenching and unclenching his
mitts, as if to make them supple. But
Sam knew the signs and said, hoarsely,
'For God's sake, Frank, don't do this.'

But Frank was clawing for his Colt
and screaming, 'To hell with you, Sam
Curry! I aim to kill you, right now!'

Frank was fanning the trigger. It was
a mistake, Sam knew, but some men

just never seem to learn. With lead hissing harmlessly past him, Sam coolly turned sideways, sighted his Colt and fired.

Frank howled as lead hit him in the right thigh. Moaning, he dropped his Colt from now nerveless fingers, bent, and with trembling hands gripped his injured leg. Blood began seeping red through Frank's fingers before dripping into the dust.

Sam slowly holstered his Colt. 'I could have killed you, Frank. Now go get that leg fixed and get back to the Blue Jay and get your thinking straight.'

'To hell with you, Sam Curry!' Frank shrieked. He stared wildly, looking up at the tops of the false fronts opposite. 'Henry, for Chris' sake, why ain't you killed the bastard yet!'

Sam realized, with all the excitement, he had temporarily forgotten that danger. He dropped to the dust and began rolling toward the boardwalk fronting the Long Bar, once more dragging out his Colt.

A rifle cracked from atop the Ace in the Hole, Vince Guthrie's place. Once, twice, three times. Sam realized lead was exploding dust off the street all around him. 'Malachi!' he yelled.

'Can't get a clear shot!'

Then Malachi went into action. His rifle spat fire twice. There was a despairing yell. A body toppled off the top of the Ace in the Hole and crashed down on to the boards of the awning covering the boardwalk. Then it smashed through the thin planks to hit the street with a bony crump.

Henry Norton did not move again.

Sam turned vicious eyes on to Frank.

'Why, you low down son of a — '

That was as far as Sam got. Frank was about to throw his Bowie knife, pulled from his boot top while Sam was distracted by the new threat from Frank's brother Henry. But Frank was too slow. Sam's lead hit him between the eyes and he died staring into the ice-blue gaze of the architect of his demise. But Frank was hardly dead when Sam realized there was another danger in the offing. Where were the rest of the Blue Jay boys? They had to be around somewhere.

He yelled at his brother, 'Get off the street, Malachi . . . into the office!'

Knowing Malachi would not need a second telling Sam made for the office. Inside the building, and Malachi by his side, Sam slammed the door, edged to the newly repaired window and stared through it, but keeping in cover.

After a couple of minutes of white-hot tension, he licked his lips. Nothing came out of the Long Bar swing doors. But there was movement behind the windows; people staring out at the dead bodies of the Norton boys on the street, as if trying to make up their minds what to do about it.

Sam wiped a slightly shaking hand across his sweat-moist lips as he continued to stare across the thorough-fare. Flies, he saw, were already landing on the bodies of Frank and Henry.

After moments, Hiram Campbell

appeared at the swing doors of the Long Bar and stepped out on to the street. First he went to have a look at Frank's body; and then he moved to Henry's carcass further down the street. After that, he turned and stared across at the law office and called, 'You have done a real job here, Sam Curry; damned if you ain't.'

Sam glared across the street. His reply was bitter. 'They brought it on themselves. But I don't owe you a damned explanation, Campbell. You must have known about this.'

'I knew nothing,' Campbell said. 'I've been in the back for an hour or more, helping to unload goods.'

Still resentful, Sam said, 'Are the rest of the Blue Jay scum in there?'

Campbell shook his head. 'Frank and Henry came in alone, early this morning. They been liquoring up all day.' He added, more as a sneer, 'That explains why they're dead and you ain't, I guess.'

Sam ignored the suggestion that Frank

sober was the better duellist and flicked a glance up the street. He saw Mal Grison and three of his deputies running down the road; Vince Guthrie was not far behind. It appeared they were all coming from the direction of City Hall. Then Sam saw Graham Eccles come bounding out of the *Scar County Clarion* office, pulling on his coat even though the temperature was topping 110° Fahrenheit. Eccles began running towards the scene of the shootings, pencil and notebook already in hand.

Seeing this activity people began filing out into the street once more, joining those who had already ventured out. Traffic started moving, too. Now close enough, Grison halted and stared at the two bodies, then turned his gaze on to Malachi and Sam, who were now standing outside the law office. Malachi was cradling his rifle across his chest.

Grison said, 'OK, Sam, what happened?'

They'd got on first name terms the week before, Sam explained and after the story was told, Grison turned to Hiram Campbell. 'Did you see it?'

The owner of the Long Bar shook his head. 'No, I did not, but I got the feeling right off Frank and Henry were in town looking for trouble.'

Vince Guthrie heaved a sigh. 'Well, it seems they found it.' He turned amber eyes on to Sam. 'A killing, Sam? This isn't usually your style.'

'I was left with no choice.' Sam stared at his friend. 'You have the office window repaired?' It was a crazy thing to be thinking about at this time, but the repair had been intriguing Sam.

Vince said, 'While you were gone. How did it go? Find anything?'

Sam shook his head. 'Not a damned thing. They're real good, Vince; best I've ever come up against.'

Sheriff Grison stared at Vince, then Sam. Grison's narrow gaze was full of curiosity before it filled with suspicion. Finally, he said, 'Dammit, what are you talking about? Is it something I should know?'

Sam stared, a little surprised. 'You ain't heard?'

Grison shook his head. 'Been on the south range, rustler trouble. Just got back an hour ago. Dammit, what's happened' — he waved a hand at the carcasses — 'apart from this?'

Graham Eccles the *Scar County Clarion* owner said, 'Malachi Curry here killed Big Mouth Bartlett night before last, right there in the Long Bar.'

Sam met Grison's astonished stare as it turned on to him. 'This true?'

Sam said, 'What Graham didn't tell you is, Malachi and me were bush-whacked out on the street. We hit one of them and followed a trail of blood we thought belonged to the bushwhacker into the Long Bar. Bartlett tried to kill me from the balcony; Malachi was just a wee bit faster and shot straighter.'

Grison stared at Hiram Campbell. 'That right?'

Campbell nodded. 'That's how it was, I guess.'

Grison looked down and paddled

about in the ankle-deep dust of the street in size ten boots. He was clearly unhappy. After moments he looked up and said, 'Sam, guess you know well as I do I'll have to take you and Malachi in until this matter is cleared up. That's my job.'

Sam stared, the grooves in his scarred face hardening. He said, 'Well, by God, you'll pay hell doing it,' he said. 'All we did was defend ourselves.'

Grison paddled in the dust again. 'Even so, it's got to be investigated!'

'Investigated, hell!' Sam said. 'What really wants investigating is that stage hold up, the murder of Meredith Seaton, the US mail taken and God knows what else that's going on in this county.'

Grison said, 'Meredith Seaton's demise is being investigated and, Sam, I don't have to remind you, US mail is chiefly your province. And, dammit, have you come up with anything yet? Do you want me to answer that?'

Sam just stared. There was no

answer. He had failed, same as Grison.

'Thought so,' the Scar County sheriff remarked. 'But that said, we searched damn near every inch of the Lonesomes to find that scum, but every trail we found petered out in those damned rocks. In the end I called in on Fort Charles and asked Major John Buckley for the loan of Kayitah, the Apache tracker they have there. You heard of him?'

Sam shook his head.

Grison said, 'Well, he's the best, but at the moment he's out on a job and won't be back for three days.'

Sam sighed heavily at the news. 'Guess that's the kind of luck that's been hitting this operation all along.' But he had to admire Grison's initiative, calling on Fort Charles for the use of one of their Indian scouts.

Vince Guthrie was talking now, a little uneasily, 'Don't rightly know how to put this to you, Sam, but the governor and the county committee are getting real impatient.' He stared at

Grison. 'And you, Mal; they're saying the lack of progress is damaging the image they want to put out regarding the county as well as the territory as a whole. They've been trying to sell it as a settled and law-abiding stretch of real estate, prime for settlement. Immigration is gradually slowing up.'

Sam stared. 'Well, too damned bad, Vince. Dammit, didn't you explain what we are up against?'

Grison glared. 'Yeah — didn't you?'

Vince shrugged. He said, 'Sure I did. I just thought you'd like to know, that's all.' Then his face turned even more sober looking. 'But there is more to it. US Marshal Tim May is getting real uneasy about the theft of that mail. Real serious in his eyes and he asked me to pass on to you that he's looking for results, solid results. Sam, he is firmly of the opinion it is the cowboys that took the mail and he wants you to take the gloves off with them; he's wondering why you haven't already done so.'

Grison interceded, 'They ain't holding up stages and they ain't stealing mail. I'll bet money on it.'

Sam said, 'I've been talking to quite a few cowboys of late, Vince, and I'm coming round to the conclusion it's not them that is seriously involved in the stage hold ups. Rustling, yes, and maybe a little maverick road agenting like the one Arkansas Jack Reed tried to pull in Manteca Pass, but not serious like payrolls. Whoever it is that is doing this, well, they sure seem to know when those payrolls are being conveyed, and that tells me somebody with brains is on the inside and he is welding the gang doing these hold ups into an highly organized group and they're getting real rich doing it.'

Vince raised sandy brows. He said, 'It's a possibility, I suppose, but I'm personally not convinced that is the case. I still think it's the cowboys.'

Sam said, 'Time will tell, I reckon.' He looked at the two dead bodies. 'Well, I guess it's time to get that garbage off the streets and back to the Blue Jay.'

169

Vince stared. 'Are you intending to take them? Is that wise?'

Sam shook his head. 'No, it ain't wise, but that is what I intend to do.'

Grison said, 'You will be unduly antagonizing them, Sam. Let them come in. Why make even bigger enemies of them?'

Sam stared and said, 'No, I'm sick of waiting for things to happen. I intend to start making things happen instead.'

Grison fidgeted in the dust with the points of his size ten boots, then seemed to come to a decision. 'Let me deal with it,' he said. 'I'll explain to John and Haines it was a fair fight, that you tried to talk Frank out of it.'

Sam shook his head. 'No. I want to look them in the eye, impress on them the good times are over.'

Vince said, 'Don't be a damn fool, Sam, leave it to Mal. Why take undue risks?'

Sam stared at his friend. 'How long did we work together, Vince? Ten years? You should know by now that I like to meet trouble head on. That's how I am

170

and I can't change now.'

After being quiet for so long Malachi said, grinning, 'You can count me in, brother. I liked the old times.'

Vince sighed and loudly slapped his big hands against the sides of his thighs and said, 'Well, hell, go on, get yourselves killed if that's what you want. I'm through.'

Grison mopped his brow. 'Figure it won't come to that.' He turned and Sam met his gaze. Grison said, 'I'll send a deputy with you, Sam, let him explain the situation. Maybe the Blue Jay will respect that and keep their guns in their holsters. Given half the chance, John Wright can be a reasonable man.'

Vince growled, 'Well, I'm going back to the office — too damned hot out here.' He went pacing off, up the street.

Grison said, staring at Sam, 'I'll send along that deputy.'

'Fair enough, Mal.'

Meantime, Graham Eccles owner and editor of the *Scar County Clarion* scribbled vigorously.

11

The setting sun was painting the thin, sparse clouds yellow, orange and red above the dark peaks of the Lonesome Mountains as Sam, Malachi and Deputy Sheriff Roland Smiley splashed across Black Water Creek. Grim-faced now, the three men rode up the gentle slope to the long, low adobe Blue Jay ranch house.

Malachi was leading Frank's big roan and Henry's smaller paint. Each dead man was draped over his own horse and roped down. The three men had taken turns to do the task on the trail to here, Malachi taking the final stretch.

The place was as quiet as a tomb: no smoke rose from the chimneystack, no hands lounged about the yard, waiting for supper. Sam's uneasiness grew. It was damned uncanny, this lack of human activity.

With Malachi and Smiley he reined in his roan before the six-horse tie rail. Malachi was looking round charily while chewing lazily on his chaw. Then he spat and said, 'Where the hell is everybody?'

Roland Smiley said, 'Unusual, it's got to be said.'

Sam dismounted cautiously, tied up and stepped up on to the stoop, crossed it and pushed at the door. It swung open on squeaking iron hinges. He called, 'The house?' But silence persisted, except for the screech of an eagle high overhead. Uneasy now, Malachi and Roland Smiley dismounted and stared around. Eventually, Smiley said, loosening his Colt Army in its holster,

'I'll go take a look in the barns and bunkhouse.'

'Be careful.' Sam said. Then he looked at Malachi. 'Let's search the house.'

He cautiously entered the big living room. It stank of Mexican food and rank men, but the place had been tidied up, though not thoroughly. It was then a woman came into the room from the passage to the left. She was a Pima squaw by the look of her, Sam decided, but with no real certainty. They near all looked the same to him, the women of these Southwest tribes: round face, black intense eyes, black hair, black dress with a silver-decorated belt around the middle.

Sam stared at her. 'Where are the men?'

'They gone.'

'When?'

'This morning.' She shook her head. 'Frank and Henry not go, went to Columbus.'

Sam said, 'Where did the rest of them go?'

She shrugged. 'They go. They no tell me.'

'When will they be back, do you know?'

The Pima woman hunched her shoulders. 'They come, they go; I make food, they eat. That's all.'

'She's lying!' Malachi said.

He stepped closer and looked meanly at the woman. Then he slapped the quirt in his hand against his greasy buckskin trousers. 'Leave her with me for five minutes, brother. She'll tell then, by God.'

Sam stared. 'There'll be none of that stuff, Malachi, I'll handle it.'

His brother scowled. 'You're too damned easy, allus was.'

Sam said, 'We'll see.' He turned to the squaw. 'We could do with some food, woman. We've had a long ride.'

The squaw's shiny, deep brown face was expressionless. She waved a hand towards a passageway to their left. She said, 'Food in there, but I no ask you to eat. John beat me if I ask you. No want beat. Get enough beat. You tell John, if he ask — but you take, I no ask.'

'Don't worry about it,' Sam said.

He looked at Malachi. They walked down the passageway, past two bedrooms with blankets still strewn on the floor and on into a large kitchen. Ever since entering the house Sam had smelt the spicy aromas of chilli con carne and there it was simmering on the big stove in the far corner. It reminded him of home, of the *Hacienda San Luis* and of his wife Consuelo's exquisite cooking. Pangs of longing scurried through him making him realize how much he was missing Consuelo and the children, though he had tried to put the longing at the back of his mind.

Roland Smiley walked into the kitchen.

'Nothing in the barns,' he said. 'The place is dead.'

Sam sat down. Malachi brought over the huge pan of stew from off the big range and set it on the table and sat down. Bowls and spoons were already placed on the rough, but scrubbed, pine boards.

Smiley sat down with a grin when he realized what was happening. 'That's more like it. Man, I could eat a horse.'

He helped himself to stew. Soon, all were eating. After a minute's silence

Sam said, looking at the deputy, 'Have you any ideas as to where they are? The squaw won't tell. D'you know their habits?'

The deputy shrugged. 'Beats me; but then, the Wrights have always been a law unto themselves.'

'Take a guess,' Sam said.

'They have horses in the hills. Maybe they've had an order from the army and are on a roundup.'

Sam stared at the deputy. 'You don't seriously believe that.'

'Why not? They're horse traders.'

'They're also cow thieves,' Sam said.

Smiley stared at him. 'Catching your drift you're wanting me to say what *you're* thinking, uh? That they're in Mexico borrowing cattle.'

Malachi said, 'Fits the bill, don't it?'

Smiley took in a spoonful of stew, chewed and then said, 'Well, I guess they do have a reputation for it — Don Alonzo Abello's herd in particular. Abello claims John and his boys are robbing him blind and he wants something done about it. But he keeps quiet about killing old man Wright down there last year, though the Wright boys did kill four of Abello's *vaqueros* in the fracas. And John and James still claim they were on legitimate business, that they were attacked and it was murder, but that story ain't generally believed.'

Sam said, 'What have you been doing about it?'

Smiley stared. 'Well, hell, we can't do a damn thing till we catch them crossing the line with cattle bearing Don Alonzo's mark. Though, I got to say, we ain't been making much of an effort in that direction, what with all these other things going on elsewhere — miners playing up, highway robbery and the like.'

More silence. The twilight faded fast and the squaw, sitting in the corner watching them until now, rose and lit a lamp and placed it on the table. Then she stared at Sam. 'You finished now?' she said. 'You go now?'

Sam pushed his empty bowl away and said, 'We're staying until John and his boys turn up, woman.' He stared at the other two men. 'Better do something with Frank and Henry and turn the horses into the corral, water and feed them.'

Smiley volunteered to attend to the horses and Sam and Malachi dealt with Frank and Henry Norton, lying the two bodies side by side on the dirt floor of the smaller of the two barns.

Returning to the house Sam found a comfortable chair in the common room and spread out. Malachi made himself as cosy as possible on the floor. It was then Deputy Smiley popped his head through the open door to say he would sleep in the hay in the larger barn. The Pima woman shuffled in from the back at that moment and said she had a cot in the out-house and they could find her there if they wanted her. Deep quiet now descended over the Blue Jay ranch house. Only a coyote was singing its lonely serenade to the mountains.

12

Sam awakened to hear the faint sound of a walking horse. He instantly became fully alert and rose. Through the dirty window he saw a thin crescent of moon was now shining silver-pale in the star-studded sky. The coyote had stopped its howling but way out in the mountains the wolves were chorusing.

The walking horse came on until the soft clop of its hoofs stopped. A man, clearly hurt, was slumped in the saddle, head resting on his chest. Sam eased out his Colt. Malachi was now awake and staring up at him. Without a sound, his brother got up and drew his Smith & Wesson and joined him. It was then a voice called from outside. It was pleading and full of pain.

'Teresa!'

The Pima squaw came bustling through the big room and out through the plain board door. Then Sam heard her say, '*Patrón*! What has happened?'

The injured man's head came up, slowly and Sam saw it was John Wright. Teresa, the Pima woman, was trying to help him down.

Sam stepped out. He eased her aside and helped the eldest Wright to the ground. Lying there, John looked up at him and then slew his gaze to Malachi, who was now standing behind Sam's knee-bent form. Pain made John's stare bright. Sam saw he had three wounds: one in the right shoulder, one in the calf, and one in the stomach. And John Wright had bled considerably; that was plain.

Deputy Roland Smiley came out of the large barn and joined them. He stared down at the part owner of the Blue Jay. It was then that John Wright groped out with a hand and grasped Sam's arm. He pulled him close and stared up, trying to focus his eyes. 'That Sam Curry? What the hell are you doing here?'

Sam said, 'That'll keep for now. What happened, John? Where are the rest of your boys?'

Wright slumped back, stared at the stars. 'We were ambushed. Walked right into it. Crazy.'

'Where?'

'El Trento Pass.'

Sam said, 'Mexico? What were you doing down there?' He asked it, even though he knew it was a damn fool question.

Despite his hurts Wright's lips formed a bloody grin. He said, 'Jesus, Curry, what the hell d'you think we were doing?'

'Who did it?'

Wright gasped for a few moments as though more pain was assailing him. Then he said, 'Got to be Don Alonzo, though I could swear he had some *Rurales* with him.'

'You sure?'

'No, dammit, but Abello's had it in for us for a while.'

'Where are the rest of you?'

'Dead. Like I say, we walked right into it. Never stood a chance.'

Sam said, 'You sure they're all dead?'

John stared up, hard. 'Sure I'm sure. Would I say it if I weren't sure? Dammit, I saw it all. A miracle *I* got out alive.'

'Wild Man Haines?'

'Hit on the first volley. They sure had it in for *him*!'

'Your brothers, James, Jeff?'

'Both dead.'

The squaw, Teresa, said, 'I think you dead soon, too, *patrón*. I go now. No use for Pima squaw here anymore. Go back to Gila, Maricopa Wells.'

Fire kindled in John Wright's eyes. He stared fiercely at Teresa. 'The hell you will, woman! You stay here, y'hear? I ain't dead yet!'

The squaw bowed her head, seemed to shrink a little and then she stepped back and shrugged. 'OK. I wait. Dead pretty soon. You see.'

John glared and snorted, 'Damned woman!' He switched his gaze on to

Sam again. 'An' you, you ain't said why you're here, yet. Spill it.'

'Frank and Henry Norton, they're dead. They came into town looking for trouble. They got it.'

The lines in John Wright's face, already etched by pain, hardened into anger. 'I told the dumb bastards how it would be! But would they listen?' Deep melancholy now seemed to fill the eldest Wright. 'Don't seem right,' he said presently, 'all of us gone. Man, we had a real good thing going . . . real good.'

Sam said, 'John, you know you're dying. Go to your Maker with a clean heart. Did you kill my brother Arthur?'

Fire again kindled for a moment in John Wright's eyes as he stared up. 'Dammit! I told you; we had nothing to do with it!'

Sam said, 'Vince Guthrie says otherwise.'

'Well that damned son of a bitch is wrong!'

Then John tried to get up but gave

out with an agonized cry. Blood spurted out of his mouth and down the front of his blue shirt. Slowly he slumped back.

'Oh! Jesus!'

After a moment or two Sam felt John's grip on his coat sleeve tighten. 'You figure I'm going to die, Sam?'

'Seems to me you asked for all you got, John, and you're heading for the big Roundup in the Sky.'

Something akin to hurt came to John Wright's gaze then it hardened to become fierce anger. 'By God, allus did have you marked down for a no good son of a bitch, Sam Curry!'

More blood ran from his mouth and he flopped back. Sam felt his hand release its hold on his sleeve as breath began to shudder out of him. It wasn't long before the spark of life slowly left John's grey unblinking stare. Now the pulse of the carotid artery faded and John Wright became still.

Roland Smiley said, after a few quiet moments, 'For all his faults, he was a game bastard.'

But Malachi's thoughts were clearly on other matters as he said, 'Do you believe him, Sam — about Arthur I mean?'

Sam shrugged. 'A man don't usually lie in the face of his own death.'

'I've known men lie through their back teeth, dying or not,' Malachi said with the bitterness of long experience.

Sam raised brows. 'Me, too, but I got the feeling not this time.' He stared at his brother through the weak silver moonlight. 'Know what, Malachi? I reckon we're still looking for Arthur's killer.'

At this point the Pima squaw started walking into the night, toward the smaller barn, saying as she went, 'Nothing here for Teresa now.'

Roland Smiley stared after her for moments then said, 'Gents, I guess we've got some burying to do.'

'Leave the scum to the coyotes,' Malachi said. 'I'm for riding. I hanker for a real bed, not those damn boards in there.'

Sam ignored him and turned to

Smiley. 'Least we can do, I guess, seeing as there is nobody else.'

'Aw, shit, Sam,' Malachi said. 'Hard one minute, soft the next; never did figure you out, dammit.'

They found spades, hitched up a flat bed wagon and threw the spades and the bodies of Frank and Henry Norton and John Wright into it. Smiley then drove half a mile up to the top of the low hill above the Blue Jay. Smiley explained it was the place the Wright's used as their family burial plot. An hour later they patted down stony soil and wiped sweat off their brows and stretched their backs. They were coming back down the hill when they saw the Pima woman in the moon-silvered distance, driving a buckboard and heading west. Sam saw the wagon was filled with a variety of goods. A small pinto was in the shafts. Teresa did not even look their way and none of them suggested they make an effort to stop her.

In the largest barn they parked up the wagon, turned the horse into the corral, forked in hay and topped up the trough. No doubt the bank, or somebody, would send men out here to deal with legal things tomorrow.

Malachi said, 'It's back to town now, right?'

'I was hoping to be heading for the *Hacienda San Luis* come noon,' Sam said, 'but with John saying they had nothing to do with Arthur's murder . . . well, now I ain't so sure.'

Malachi said, his voice more of a growl, 'Wright's lying. Arthur's killers are where they belong. Dead.'

Deputy Roland Smiley said, 'I always figured it was the Wright bunch, though Mal don't agree.'

Sam dug his heels in. 'I'm with Mal.'

Malachi glared, clearly exasperated. 'Dammit, Sam, they done it; now let's get out of here.'

Sam didn't argue. Malachi seemed to have made his mind up, so had Roland Smiley. He mounted and along with the other two urged his horse into a mile-eating canter towards Columbus.

13

It was noon by the time they got into Columbus. Smiley veered off toward City Hall — to report the slaughter to Grison, he said. The sheriff's office was on the second floor. Meantime, Sam and Malachi steered their tired mounts into the shade of Ed Brown's stables and wearily climbed down.

Sam said, 'The usual for the horses, Ed.'

Brown, his grin revealing his crooked tobacco-stained teeth, said, 'You boys look as though you've been to a funeral.'

'I guess you could call it that,' Sam said, his tiredness revealing itself in his voice. He pulled his Winchester out of its saddle scabbard and prepared to leave but Ed Brown remained staring at him, clearly disappointed. He said, 'Well, hell, you ain't going to leave it there, are you?'

Sam formed his face into a dust-stained smile. He saw no reason why the news of the Wright gang's bloody demise in El Trento Pass should not be broadcast. For, truth be known, it was probably already on the streets of Columbus, told while Roland Smiley was making his way to City Hall. The tale told, Ed Brown stared his disbelief. Then his face filled with sheer delight as he said, eagerly, 'Did you say the whole damned lot of them was killed; nary a one of them left living?'

'That's how John told it,' Sam said.

Ed's wizened eyes rounded. 'Jesus, holy cow!'

As if bored by the conversation Malachi yawned and stretched and said, 'Well, I'm heading for the sack.' He stared meaningfully at Sam. 'I'll be at Sadie Thompson's if you want me afore breakfast tomorrow.' Sadie Thompson's boarding house, Sam knew, was at the north end of town.

Sam nodded. 'I'll make a report to Vince and then bed down myself.'

Malachi grunted his reply and walked out into the furnace-hot early afternoon heat that was holding Columbus in its blistering embrace.

Ed Brown was saying, with great excitement, 'Well, for sure, those Wright boys have been asking for it. But it'll play hell with relations on both sides of the border. Ain't no love lost there, ever.'

Sam said, 'I would not dispute that.'

However, he decided, after eight years of residence down there it would not affect his position. He was now fully absorbed into that society. And he'd lay a bet that in six months' time the Wright gang's comeuppance at El Trento Pass would hardly raise an eyebrow. It would be just another statistic to add to the long and bloody history of the border.

He looked at the old stableman, felt generous and flipped him a quarter. 'Go buy yourself a drink, Ed.'

Catching the coin Brown grinned. 'No need to ask twice on that one! Here's to you, Sam Curry!'

In the mayor's office at City Hall, Sam, seated in the chair the other side of the desk, stared across its shiny top at Vince Guthrie. Guthrie was saying, clear dismay on his face:

'The whole bunch of them . . . dead?'

'That's the way John reported it.'

Vince wiped sweat off his broad forehead with a white handkerchief. The heat in the office was stifling. 'Jesus Holy Christ!' he said. Then he added with a shake of his head, 'But, for sure, they've been asking for it long enough.'

'That's what I keep hearing, and I've no reason not to believe it,' Sam said. 'But, on the other hand, John Wright also said, when I asked him, that he and his boys had nothing to do with Arthur's death and d'you know what, Vince? I believe him.' Guthrie stared with amber eyes and leaned forward, disbelief on his face. 'You can't be serious. Sam . . . John was a no good lying son of a bitch, as were the rest of that thieving bunch.'

'It was a deathbed confession, Vince,' Sam said. 'A man can be real honest when the time comes to meet his Maker. Maybe John thought if he declared his innocence here on earth, that would buy him a surefire ticket into heaven.'

Vince leaned back, his look of astonishment making his feelings clear. 'Sam, you know as well as I do, his sort will lie through their eyeteeth, even when they're dying! They've lied all their lives; they know no other way. They would not know what the truth was if it looked them in the face. And with your experience . . . man, I sure am surprised you even asked the son of a bitch the question!'

'Even so . . . ' Sam said. He looked intently at his friend. 'Vince, is there anybody else you know that had reason to kill Arthur?'

Vince gave out an exasperated sigh now and said, 'No, dammit, I don't. I told you when you arrived it were John

Wright or some of his boys — more than likely the Norton brothers — and I'm sticking to that. And I'm not the only one in town who believes that.'

Sam said, 'So you really do figure the job done?'

Vince nodded his head vigorously and said, 'Yes, I do.' He got up and came around the desk smiling and rested his hand on Sam's shoulder. 'Go home, Sam, back to the San Luis, Arthur has been laid to rest.'

Sam rubbed his chin. 'Like nothing better than to do that, but I just got this feeling, Vince. But even if I hadn't my job isn't done here, yet. I also made a commitment to US Marshal Tim May and the county authorities to help chase down the road agents that are operating in the area. Dammit, you passed me the word.'

Vince waved a dismissive arm. 'Oh! I can smooth that over, no trouble. Sam, get back to Consuelo and your two children, your job here is done.'

Sam again felt Vince's friendly hand

press on his shoulder. 'Get back to the *Hacienda San Luis*, old friend, and when you get there give Consuelo my best regards.' His smile broadened as he added, 'But don't leave without calling in on the Ace in the Hole — I got a couple of toys for the children.'

Sam chewed his bottom lip. He found his resolve uncharacteristically weakening. 'You make it sound real tempting.'

'Only because the job's done.' Vince paused before he added, 'Just out of curiosity, what does Malachi think about the situation?'

Sam said, 'He thinks like you.'

Vince gave a nod of satisfaction. 'So there you have it. Sam, get the hell back home and start living again.'

Sam stared. 'You don't understand, Vince. I can't . . . loose ends, you see. I don't like loose ends.'

'Loose ends, what loose ends; they're all tied up!' Vince shook his head, as if in despair of his friend. 'Stubborn as a mule; always was.' He sighed and waved an apparently dismissive hand. 'OK,' he said, 'go get yourself killed, dammit, an' see if I care.'

Sam said, with feeling, 'That's one thing I do know for sure, Vince, and that is you do care. And I'll always be grateful for that.'

Vince 'humphed' and went back to his seat.

Sam rose from his chair and left the building. He headed for Mary Summerbee's quiet rooming house on Fourth Street. Sleep was a desperate need in him now and after a bath and some food (he was sure Mary Summerbee would oblige) he would sleep the night through.

After that: *Quién Sabe?* Who knows?

14

Mid-morning next day found Sam walking up the boardwalk lining Main Street fully refreshed after fourteen hours of almost uninterrupted sleep. He was heading for the Long Bar, Hiram Campbell's place. Campbell seemed to have been friendly with the Wright boys when they were alive and Sam wanted to pump the Long Bar owner for what he knew about that outlaw bunch, if they actually could have killed Arthur, or had reason to do.

Main Street was real busy, chocked full of huge ox-drawn ore wagons heading for the stamping mills, plus cowboys and farming families in for materials and provisions or to just plain quench a thirst. Dust drifted heavily on the hot air and Sam wanted to get out of its rank smell.

But three gunshots sounding like the

cracks of a whiplash on the morning air brought him to a stop. He quickly deduced the firing was coming from the Ace in the Hole, his friend Vincent Guthrie's place.

He quickened his step, forgetting the Long Bar and Hiram Campbell for now. Fifty yards on he strode in through the open doors of the Ace in the Hole. His Colt was out and held ready to fire, for he did not know what to expect. What he did find stopped him in his tracks. Vince was bending over the body of Malachi, by one of the many gaming tables. Sam almost ran to his friend's side. 'God Almighty, what happened, Vince?'

His long time *amigo* looked up at him. He shook his head slowly. He looked a little bewildered. 'I don't know. I was in the office. There was shooting. I came out . . . Jesus, Sam, I'm real sorry. Malachi could be wild, but a man could not help liking him.'

Sam stared at the shocked faces of the men gathered around. They were all clearly appalled by what had occurred. 'Anybody know?' His voice was harsh, like rough sandpaper across wood. He singled out the pale-faced man he knew to be Fred Claybacker, one of the house gamblers seated at the poker table Malachi must have been playing at. 'You know?'

Outrage and disbelief in his voice, Claybacker said, 'We've been playing all night. Malachi was on a winning streak. He was ready to break it up when dawn came but the boys wanted a chance to win back their money. Well, you know Malachi. He was up for it, said he would skin us for the rest of our cash, if that was what we wanted.'

Sam's face was a tight mask. 'Then what?'

Claybacker pointed to a door at the rear of the long room. 'The shots came from over there. Malachi slumped over, bleeding, then fell to the floor.'

Pausing, Claybacker looked around at the other three players still at the table. He waved a hand. 'For a second or two we all wondered what the hell was happening, then, as you would expect, we all got down thinking we were going to be next. By the time we gathered our wits again it was clear it was all over and the bastard had hightailed it. Then Vince came in.'

Sam said, 'Why didn't anybody go after him?'

Vince said, 'Jesus, Sam, it didn't happen but a minute ago.'

Sam paced across the room to the door indicated. It was closed. Vince was close behind him. His friend said, with some anxiousness, 'Easy, Sam. It's a storeroom. He could be waiting.'

Sam didn't reply. Using the protection of the jamb he leaned over, turned the doorknob and pushed. The door creaked open on dry iron hinges. There was no sound of shots, as Sam half expected, only the scraping of chairs as men behind him strove to get out of the line of fire, just in case there was any.

Taking a deep breath, Sam bent low and scurried into the storeroom, Colt lined up and ready. Crates big and small filled the gloomy interior. The killer could be behind any one of those boxes and Sam wheeled around, gun extended, ready to fire at anything that moved. But still no shots came and Sam hurried to the door leading out to the alley at the back of the Ace in the Hole.

Here he halted again. Vince was right behind him. Sam turned. Vince was clutching a Derringer twin barrel in his right hand. Sam assumed it must be from that spring-loaded contraption he knew Vince always carried, strapped to his gun arm. Sam remembered gratefully, in the old days, it had proved to be useful in many a tight spot. Sam sized up the back of the door. He saw it was hinged to swing inwards. Impatient now to get on with it, he pulled it open and dived out.

He hit the ground rolling through the ankle-deep dust and dried horse dung. Coming up against the wall of a tarpaper shack opposite he stared up and down the back alley. The passage was empty. Then the thunder of hoofs came from some hundred yards up the narrow alley. Streets crossed up there — streets just wide enough to take a wagon. He scrambled to his feet and began running.

Coming up on the corner he went round it, Colt held in two hands and extended, ready to fire. The rider was disappearing down the back road toward the Mexican quarter. He gave chase, running down the narrow lanes between the adobes, scattering dirty, brown-eyed kids that had just evaded the flying hoofs of the son of a bitch in front.

On the edge of the adobe village Sam stopped and stared at the receding rider, whose banner of dust was strung out behind him.

Vince came panting up. 'That had to be him,' he said.

Sam nodded, his face grim. 'Had to be.'

Vince said, 'What are you aiming to do now?'

Sam stared his disbelief that such words had just come from a friend and colleague of the old lawman days. 'Go after the son of a bitch, what else?'

Vince nodded, looked a little sheep-faced. 'Yeah, what else, and I'm just sorry I can't be in on it, Sam, but right now I got business commitments that can't wait.'

It wasn't the answer Sam was hoping to hear now Malachi was dead. 'I'd like you with me, Vince,' he said. 'Can't your commitments wait for a while?'

Vince stared at him looking injured by the quiet inference that his business interests should take a back seat right now. He said, 'Dammit, Sam, don't you think I want to? Hell, Malachi meant a lot to me, you know that — as you do. But it's just not possible right now.'

Sam stared at his friend. 'It ain't?'

He holstered his Colt and turned on his heel.

Vince was at his side, holding his arm. 'Hell, Sam, don't rub it in. It's bad enough for me as it is. Dammit, Mal

Grison will be forming a posse . . .
can't you wait for that? It's not as
though you need to ride out alone.'

Sam gazed at his old friend. He made
no attempt to hide his disappointment
although he did smile, vaguely. 'You
know me, Vince; can't waste a minute.'

'Be reasonable, dammit,' Vince said,
now clearly hurt. 'Wait for Grison.'

Sam said, 'I ain't feeling reasonable
right now.' He strode towards town but
aware that Vince was staring after him,
his shoulders slumped.

15

Luck sometimes does favour a man. Sam stared at the back of the White Mountain Apache, Kayitah, riding a few yards ahead of him, head down as if he was sleeping. But Sam knew Kayitah was far from that; he was deeply concentrated on the trail he was following — the trail Malachi's killer left behind.

As promised, the commander at Fort Charles had sent Kayitah to help the law in Scar County track down the now increasingly troublesome road agents. However, it took some heated haggling before Sheriff Mallory Grison finally agreed to let Kayitah go with Sam, and then only on the provision they leave a trail to follow and not to take action until the whole posse was available to deal with it. Sam found he could live with that. And the general feeling was one of excitement; everyone thought they could be on to something here.

Kayitah had picked up the trail of the killer easily. Now, mid-afternoon, they were approaching the Lonesome Mountains, ranked dark and grim ahead. Sam already knew what a beautiful, but absolute hell-hole it was when it came to the matter of following sign. Even so, with Kayitah up ahead he was feeling more than optimistic when he topped up his canteen at the first brook they hit in the foothills.

Now, an hour before sunset, they were into the cottonwood and sycamore-clad valleys of the Lonesomes. The higher slopes soared all around them, becoming pine clothed and majestic before they poked bare, black snow-streaked tops into the still brilliant afternoon sky.

It was around this time Kayitah began to grow uneasy. He slowed his buckskin pony to a stop. Sam had already learnt that Kayitah could speak good English. He drew close to the waiting Apache and stared into those black glittering eyes, which were set into a dark, fierce, aquiline face. Kayitah said, 'Him near.'

Sam did not question how Kayitah came to know that. He accepted it and gave the surrounding countryside an even closer scrutiny than he had already subjected it to. However, far as he could see, there was nothing to be concerned about. It was just steeply rising woodland basking in the warm evening sunlight.

Nevertheless, he said, 'What do you suggest?'

'We break up. Get him in two minds.'

Kayitah pointed to the rocky ridge they were heading for, maybe a mile or so up the steep, boulder-strewn cottonwood and sycamore-clad gradient before melding into dark pines. Kayitah was pointing at a lightning-shattered tree stump standing like a melancholy scarecrow atop the summit. He said, 'If nothing happens, meet me by shattered pine, hour from now.'

Sam nodded. 'As you want it.'

Kayitah grunted and turned his buckskin pony, continuing to follow the killer's tracks. Soon he was invisible amongst the thick greenery. It was then Sam turned his roan to take the left flank up the ridge side, guiding the beast through the rocks and tree boles. But there was eeriness everywhere and a towering silence that he found unnatural. It caused a cold feeling to prickle up his backbone. It set his animal instincts working overtime, his blue stare probing every suspect rock and clump of bush he could see ahead.

Ten minutes on, he thought he saw something moving — a flickering through the trees up front. It could be a man or it could be some critter. He would not take the chance.

He carefully edged his horse into cover and took a fresh grip on the Winchester in his sweat-greasy right hand.

After minutes of careful scrutiny he began to curse his edginess. There was nothing up there. He began to ease the horse upwards again, seeing through the gaps in the canopy the sky deepening and colouring, suggesting the beginnings of one of those red, gold and yellow sunsets this country is famous for.

At last he found a gap in the trees sufficient enough to allow his gaze to search the top of the ridge he and Kayitah were heading for. He tried to pick out the shattered tree stump the Apache scout had suggested they use as their rendezvous point. He found it and began to pick his way up the slope towards it.

The sudden crash of guns ahead startled him and caused him to react like a startled mule deer. He leapt off his horse dragging his Winchester out of its saddle scabbard to take shelter behind a tree bole, then immediately felt a fool. The shooting was way ahead of him, off to his right and certainly not directed at him. What the noise did suggest was that Kayitah must have found the killer, or the killer had found

Kayitah and that could be serious.

Sam shed his caution. He remounted and urged the roan toward the commotion. But the ground was difficult. It was rough, rocky and in parts the trees were close enough together to cause him to make detours. And that needled him for the sound of shots, though more spaced and selective now, were still echoing across the mountains. But, at least, the renewed shooting gave him some reassurance: Kayitah must still be alive, but in what condition?

Sam figured he was close now; the prickling feeling he was getting up his backbone was telling him so. And he could also smell the acrid stench of spent gun-powder, see the blue smoke of it like will-o-the-wisp drifting towards him through the dark pine trees ahead.

Sam eased back on the roan. There was a kind of bluff ahead, sticking out like the prow of a ship from the craggy ridge he was heading for. Then he saw that a man was crouched on the edge of the bluff, rifle held ready. He was peering intently into the trees below him.

Sam quickly established it was not Kayitah: this man was white. The last of the sunset was bathing the fellow's blue trousers and dark range coat with orange-red light. The lurid rays made him look almost luminescent and it was flashing garish light off the silver roundels attached to the man's hatband.

Eager anticipation in him now, Sam climbed down off his roan and ground hitched it. He settled behind a boulder and sighted up his Winchester. He already had a round jacked into the breech. He lined up on the man's heart region, but then paused. He must not kill him. He wanted information and that son of a bitch must possess it in buckets.

Altering his sighting, Sam squeezed off, trusting his marksmanship to hit the spot he aimed for — the right shoulder, high up. The Winchester barked, crisp and clean. The echoes scurried across the mountain vastness like the cracks of a repeatedly snapped bullwhip growing fainter all the time.

Sam heard the man's harsh cry. He was rearing up, clutching the spot Sam aimed for. But the killer was teetering on the edge of the bluff, striving mightily to save himself. Sam now found himself willing the man to hold his balance, not to fall, but the stones under his boots were giving way. With a despairing scream he toppled over the edge of the bluff and tumbled down forty feet before crashing head first on to the rocks littered about the escarpment's base. At this point Kayitah materialized to stand near the edge of the bluff top. He whooped what Sam supposed was an Apache cry of triumph and waved his Sharps carbine above his head. It was quickly becoming clear to Sam that Kayitah, after the first clash, had found cover and climbed up unseen to get behind the killer while he was shooting at shadows. Sam just happened to get there first to make the telling shot.

Sam returned the salute and mounted

his roan and picked his way up to the base of the bluff, right to where the killer had landed. He climbed down again and looked at the man who must be responsible for killing Malachi. He was dead, his skull caved in by the impact of his fall against hard rock. He was a complete stranger.

Five minutes on Kayitah joined him. The White Mountain scout looked down at the man, his dark face impassive. Then he said, with arrogant dismissal, 'Him dead for sure. We make camp; can't see to trail in dark.'

Sam stared at him. 'You think there's more?'

Kayitah shrugged. 'Think, yes — soon find out for sure.'

Sam found some comfort in that. Then, despite the bitterness and anger he felt, he heaped rocks on the body of the killer of Malachi but said no prayers. After that he rode out with Kayitah and, when the last of the sunset faded and the deep purple of starlit night set in, they made camp.

16

Next morning, after a breakfast made with the last of Mary Summerbee's beef and dark brown bread, along with mugs of strong coffee, Kayitah surprised him. 'Last night, found camp; maybe camp killer was heading for.'

Sam stared. 'You've been out?' He had not heard a thing and he prided himself on his alertness, even when sleeping.

Kayitah said, 'Uh, huh.'

'Are men there?'

'No men.' Kayitah waved a piece of paper he fished out of a pocket in his army tunic.

'Just note, you read. No understand white man's writing.'

Kayitah handed over the missive. Sam read it. '*Moved camp to Boise Canyon. Boss said be there by sunup.*'

Sam looked up and stared at the

Apache scout. 'D'you know Boise Canyon?'

Kayitah nodded. 'I know.'

Sam nodded. 'Well, that's where we're heading.'

Kayitah grunted his reply.

Sam scribbled a note and placed it prominently for Grison to find when he arrived here with the posse — they had laid a clear trail for the posse to follow. Then he moved out, following Kayitah.

Two hours on and through some pretty but tortuous country, they were now riding in more pleasant circumstances, under the shade of aspens, sycamore and cottonwoods distributed down the lower, easier slopes of the Lonesomes. It was as hot as all hell down here after the chill of last night, up in the high country.

'Boise Canyon ahead,' Kayitah said after two hours of silence. He added, 'See man on rocks?'

Almost imperceptibly Kayitah nodded toward the gap three hundred yards ahead of them. Each side of the canyon Sam saw there were ramparts of rock very suitable for ambush. He allowed his gaze to search those crags and though the fellow was well hidden, Sam finally spotted him.

He said, 'I see him.'

'We fool him, uh?' Kayitah said.

Sam stared at the Apache, making his scepticism apparent. 'I'd sure like to hear this one, Kayitah.'

The tracker gave what passed for an Apache grin. He pointed to his left. 'I go that way, you go that way.' He pointed to the right. 'Son of bitch can't look two ways, huh, Sam Curry?'

Sam thought: Apache logic? He immediately saw the flaw in the plan, but, damn on damn, Kayitah was already urging his buckskin pony across the dry, curly short grass to eventually turn in toward the rear of the bluff the lookout was on.

'Kayitah!' Sam called after him. 'It won't work.'

But there was no response from the Apache and, as Sam expected, the lookout fired three warning shots into the pristine blue sky. Then he began scrambling down the bluff side to the entrance to Boise Canyon. Soon he was mounted and galloping away, to disappear from sight over the brow of the rise.

Sam now saw Kayitah, as soon as he realized what was happening, turn his mount, hauling on the reins as cruelly as only an Apache can. Kicking knee-length moccasin heels hard into the pony's flanks, he rode back to rejoin Sam. He was clearly disappointed. When he got close, he said, 'Asshole run.'

Sam glared. 'What the hell you expect?'

Kayitah shrugged. 'That he fight, maybe?'

'Fat chance of that!' Sam said.

Kayitah shrugged again. 'Make mistake, it happens. Now what? Wait for posse?'

Sam continued to glare. 'You haven't left us a lot of choice. What did you do it for, anyway? Chase off like that?'

Kayitah offered his Apache grin, although it resembled a knife slash across bare brown flesh. 'Want kill white man,' he said. 'Don't often get chance to kill white man . . . legitimate, that is.'

Sam glared at the Native American. 'Son of a bitch' teetered on his lips, but he held the expletive back. Instead he said, 'Well, to hell with that. Let's go see what's on the other side of that rise.'

Kayitah grinned his delight. 'Now Sam Curry talks like warrior!'

Sam scowled. 'The hell he does, but come on anyway.'

They cantered their horses up the long, gentle slope. On its brow Sam peered down the length of Boise Canyon: calm, green and tranquil — probably not what Arizona is famous for, but it happened occasionally, he knew, and that was what made the territory so fascinating. Maybe half a mile away they saw the lookout was heading for a couple of log cabins down by the stream that was lined with clumps of willow and cottonwood. Smoke was rising from the two stone chimneystacks built into the sides of the dwellings. This appeared to be a permanent camp. Men were paused in what they had been doing, watching the rider come in. Cattle, rustled no doubt, were cropping the lush grass. Sam narrowed his eyelids. Was this the hideout of the gang that was playing hell with the payroll shipments and maybe stirring up trouble with the ranchers and sodbusters? Sam reckoned he did not even need to guess. What was significant was this had all the signs of being an organized, well-drilled outfit. Eleven, maybe twelve men were down there and it was clear a couple of them had spotted them, silhouetted as they were against the skyline.

The lookout now joined the bunch and began talking fast. It was then Sam saw Vince Guthrie coming out of one of the cabins. *Vince Guthrie?* At first, Sam did not believe his eyes, but there he was — burly of figure and purposeful of walk. However, no town clothes; Vince was in riding gear.

Two shots echoed into the mountains from behind. Gut tightening up, Sam turned in the saddle, automatically drawing his Winchester. He saw it was Mal Grison and a posse of twenty well armed men riding up the slope. Sam saw most of them were cowboys, but there were some townspeople amongst them as well. Soon they were lining up along the top of the brow alongside him and Kayitah and looking down the length of Boise Canyon. Grison eased up alongside Sam. He said:

'Found your note. Who did you bury?'

'The skunk that killed Malachi.'

'Well, now, one down.' Mallory stared down into Boise Canyon. 'Seems like we're getting somewhere, Sam.'

'Looking down there, right to the heart of it, is my guess.'

'Ain't arguing,' Grison said.

Sam could now see feverish activity

was going on around the two cabins. Sam also saw Vince Guthrie was heading for his big chestnut gelding. Reaching it he threw his saddle over it. Now he was staring up at the mouth of the canyon, shading his eyes against the sun's brassy glare. But it was only a momentary pause before he mounted and began to ride for the south wall of the canyon. Sam could not believe it was his friend of fifteen years' standing he was looking at; half of him was desperately hoping there was a reasonable explanation for this but he knew damn well there wasn't one.

Grison said, a little incredulously, 'Is that the mayor down there?'

Sam said, tersely, 'He's mine, Mal, you hear me?'

Grison stared. 'Hold on, Sam, this could be entirely innocent.'

Sam said, 'If he is innocent, why is he running?' He pulled out the note that was left near the place Malachi's killer met his end. He said, 'Read this, Mal, and then make a judgement.'

Grison read it and then looked up, surprised. 'You figure the 'boss' mentioned is Vince Guthrie?'

'Who else can it be?'

Grison was clearly shocked. 'But this is unbelievable.'

Sam said, 'I'm finding it as hard to come to terms with it myself. But the way things are looking right now it can't be anybody else. Vince has the brains, and brains have been behind the successful hold ups like Gonzalez Pass and other places — and inside knowledge. Why he is doing this we'll have to find out.'

Sam stared across the line of posse men and called, 'Hear what I said just now? Vince Guthrie is mine.'

One cowboy said, laconically, 'More'n enough to go around, Deputy; you kin have him.'

Another said, 'Some Goddamned lawman Guthrie turned out to be! Goddamned son of a bitch!'

Then all faces set into grim masks and minds concentrated on the potential bloody business ahead.

17

It was a wild run down that long slope. The men down there were now in saddles and were splitting up to go in different directions. It appeared to Sam this split had been prearranged and more than likely organized by Vince. Sam kept his eyes sighted on his friend, to the exclusion of all else.

Vince was now spurring across the stream into the trees ranked along the opposite bank. As he rode, Sam heard the guns start popping, the shouts of excited men. But his concentration was centred on Vince. He badly wanted to know how and why Vince had gotten himself into this. He felt betrayed, violated in a strange way. And if it turned out that Vince *had* been implicated in Arthur and Malachi's deaths . . . well, man, that was too awful to contemplate.

As he broke out of the streamside trees Sam saw Vince was now riding up the steep south side of the canyon. It was a narrow, hazardous climb, along what looked to be an infrequently used trail. He urged the roan up it. Fifteen minutes on, after a hair-raising climb, he watched Vince breast the canyon rim and disappear over it. A minute later he followed.

Vince was riding down the long grassy slope leading away from the ridge. He was heading towards the broken, forested country a couple of miles in the distance. Sam immediately appreciated that once Vince got into that wilderness he stood a real chance of getting away and, Sam decided, it was an even bet Vince knew it like the back of his hand. Another thing he knew: the big chestnut Vince was riding had speed and stamina and was well able to outrun his already tired roan.

There was only one thing to do.

He dismounted, drew his Winchester from its saddle scabbard. He got down on one knee, set the back sight to three hundred yards. The air was calm; no windage factor came into this. Sam waited for Vince to come into range and then he levered off two shots. Echoes quarrelled their way through the mountain vastness as he saw Vince's horse veer sideways and start biting at its mortal wounds. Then it staggered and fell heavily. Vince hit the rocky ground hard — hard enough, Sam reckoned, to stun him.

Satisfaction in him, Sam remounted, slipped the Winchester back into its scabbard and drew his Colt. Then he urged his sweating horse toward the motionless Vince Guthrie. As he got close he eyed the fallen man with great caution and then said, 'Vince?'

After moments there was a groan and Vince came over on to his back and stared up. He was bleeding from a gash in his head. He said, 'Jesus, that was a damned dirty thing to do, Sam. I thought better of you. Hell, now I feel I don't know you at all, shooting a man's horse from under him like that.'

Sam ignored the complaint and said, 'What gives, Vince? Why are you riding with this scum? Is it you behind the stage hold ups?'

Vince made a growl in his throat and stared defiantly up with those unusual amber eyes of his. After long moments, while he seemed to be debating things in his mind, he said, 'Aw, hell, knowing you, you're going to find out anyway.' Vince waved a tired hand. 'I thought I'd got it made. Everything was going swell with the Ace in the Hole, but I got over-ambitious. The OK mine — the mine I told you about — it came up for sale. Ellis Boucher owned it. Like a fool I fell for his patter despite warnings from friends.' Vince shrugged, his amber look candid. 'But I let greed and ambition have its way with me and I bought it. Sam, it turned out to be the dumbest deal I've ever made. The silver ran out in a fortnight.'

Sam said, his tone cold, bitter, 'Go on.'

Vince gave out with an ironic laugh. He said, 'Well, bad luck don't come in small packages, old buddy, that much I've learnt. We were on a quiet night in the Ace in the Hole. This guy was on a big roll; he was winning all before him. The dealer sent for me, wanting to know what limit to set. I said I'd cover all bets, confident his luck would run out — it always did. But this time it didn't and I was cleaned out, only the Ace in the Hole left in my name. I was desperate. I went to the bank; they offered me a loan to keep me going but with an interest rate near out of sight. Even so, I took it. I was determined to pick myself up, start again come hell or high water and learn the lessons.'

Once more Sam said, 'Go on.'

Vince's features hardened and became defiant. He said, 'But again things did not go as planned and I got resentful. Dammit, Sam, I put my life on the line to maintain law and order for nigh on fifteen years, taking peanut wages for doing it. Well, I figured I wasn't going to go back to that so gathered a real hard crew around me and I gave myself two years to make a real killing then get out of it.' Vince's eyes widened and became eager, almost pleading. 'You can appreciate that, can't you, Sam? It was ready made. I couldn't be in a better position, and being mayor I got to know about key deliveries. Hell, Sam, you got to understand, I was desperate.'

Sam said, calmly and evenly even though he was totally coldly angry and completely disgusted, 'The settlers, the killings, the harassment of them; were you in on that, too? Take Mary Summerbee's husband for instance . . . '

Vince looked momentarily sorry. 'Yeah, well, that shouldn't have happened. Things got out of hand. But the overall plan was good, Sam. Dammit, you got to see that. That idea was a smokescreen, to put the focus on the cowboys.' He grinned. 'Real clever, huh?'

Sickened, Sam said, 'Why did you send for me, Vince?'

Vince was sitting up now, dusting off his expensive riding gear. 'Dammit, I just felt I owed you, Sam, you know, friendship and all that stuff. I even naively figured you'd ride in, pay your respects and then go home again. I thought you would be eager to get back to Consuelo and the children, especially when I'd convinced you it was the cowboys that killed Arthur, even though nobody was going to prove it.'

'You must have known I would not settle for that.'

Vince waved a hand. 'Yeah, I recognized that — damn fool that I was — but only after you telegraphed to ask me to fix up a lawman's job for you. However, by then it was too late to put you off so I had to go through with it.'

Sam stared at his old friend, the man that had laid his life on the line for him on two occasions in the past. He did not want to ask the question, but knew he must. 'Who killed Arthur, Vince?'

Vince stared away, as if he could not bear to look at Sam, face that bitter ice-blue stare that was boring into his. Then he shrugged and returned his stare, his attitude defiant. 'Aw, what the hell? Arthur allus was too damned good at his job and he figured out what I was up to; but for old times' sake he gave me a chance, warned me to stop or he would have no recourse but to arrest me. Well, I couldn't stop; I was in too deep. But I didn't give up. I thought I could talk him round. I said I'd cut him in on the deal; said I could make him more in one year than he could earn in a lifetime doing law enforcement. But he would not listen.' Vince's stare now pleaded as it looked up. Sam was sickened by it. But Vince still had more to say. 'He *forced* me into having him killed, Sam, can't you see that?'

'Malachi? You order his death, too?'

Vince's look turned ugly when he saw the stern, unforgiving lines that had formed on Sam Curry's face and he thought: here he was, the great Sam Curry, the fellow who always got his man, made the law his God. 'Sure I did,' he said through his sneer. 'D'you know why? I knew you'd come a-running so I arranged with Malachi's killer to set an easy trail for you to follow and then hole up somewhere until you showed. But then Kayitah showed up, damn his Apache hide, and spoiled the whole damn set up.'

Hate such as he had never known now filled Sam. He wanted to kill this man. He could not bear to even think his name. However, with the terrible restraint he had always practised but for once in his life did not want to, he said, 'I'm going to have to take you in, Vince.'

Uncharacteristically for a moment like this, Vince grinned. He said, 'Sure you are, old buddy — you're Sam Curry!'

Sam watched Vince's right arm flick. He was ready for the stingy gun, hidden, he knew, in Vince's right sleeve. It was barely out of its spring-loaded hiding place and into Vince's hand when Sam brought his Colt to bear. He fired twice, triggering the weapon smoothly and efficiently. Two crimson blossoms appeared on Vince's barrel chest.

Vince's amber stare was now full of disbelief. Slowly he keeled over, his gaze still fastened on Sam's stark blue look. As Vince slumped he vaguely offered a grin, his teeth smeared with blood. He said, 'You always were too damn good!'

Sam watched him die. He had no pity in him.

Sam turned his horse to find the posse, thinking some in Scar County would find the details of this hard to believe. However, he would explain it to them as best he could. After that he would cross the border, head for the *Hacienda San Luis* — to Consuelo and the children and the good life he had found in Mexico. Though he knew his life would never be the same, at least it was now clean and the wrongs done to his family had been righted. He compressed grim lips. Perhaps at some future time there would be forgiveness?

But no, the hurt was too deep.

We do hope that you have enjoyed reading this large print book.

Did you know that all of our titles are available for purchase?

We publish a wide range of high quality large print books including:
Romances, Mysteries, Classics
General Fiction
Non Fiction and Westerns

Special interest titles available in large print are:
The Little Oxford Dictionary
Music Book, Song Book
Hymn Book, Service Book

Also available from us courtesy of Oxford University Press:
Young Readers' Dictionary
(large print edition)
Young Readers' Thesaurus
(large print edition)

For further information or a free brochure, please contact us at:
Ulverscroft Large Print Books Ltd.,
The Green, Bradgate Road, Anstey,
Leicester, LE7 7FU, England.
Tel: (00 44) **0116 236 4325**
Fax: (00 44) **0116 234 0205**

Other titles in the
Linford Western Library:

RAKING HELL

Lee Clinton

A body is wrapped in a bloodstained horse-blanket. A farmer admits to the gruesome crime, but with good reason. So will the sheriff arrest or protect the guilty man when eight men come looking to settle the score? After all, the sheriff has taken an oath to protect the town . . . This story of judgement, consequence and the promise of retribution, tells of one man — Sheriff Will Price — who is prepared to go raking hell to fulfil his pledge . . .